Charles V. Boys

Soap-Bubbles and the Forces Which Mould Them

Being a course of three lectures delivered in the theatre of the London institution

on the afternoons of Dec. 30, 1889

Charles V. Boys

Soap-Bubbles and the Forces Which Mould Them
Being a course of three lectures delivered in the theatre of the London institution on the afternoons of Dec. 30, 1889

ISBN/EAN: 9783337363642

Printed in Europe, USA, Canada, Australia, Japan

Cover: Foto ©Andreas Hilbeck / pixelio.de

More available books at **www.hansebooks.com**

· SOAP-BUBBLES ·

AND THE

FORCES WHICH MOULD THEM.

BEING A COURSE OF THREE LECTURES

DELIVERED IN THE THEATRE OF THE LONDON
INSTITUTION ON THE AFTERNOONS OF DEC. 30, 1889,
JAN. 1 AND 3, 1890, BEFORE A JUVENILE AUDIENCE.

BY

C. V. BOYS, A.R.S.M., F.R.S.,

ASSISTANT PROFESSOR OF PHYSICS AT THE ROYAL COLLEGE OF SCIENCE,
SOUTH KENSINGTON.

PUBLISHED UNDER THE DIRECTION OF THE GENERAL LITERATURE
COMMITTEE.

SOCIETY FOR PROMOTING CHRISTIAN KNOWLEDGE,
LONDON : NORTHUMBERLAND AVENUE, W.C. ;
43, QUEEN VICTORIA STREET, E.C.
BRIGHTON: 129, NORTH STREET.
NEW YORK: E. & J. B. YOUNG & CO.
1896.

TO

G. F. RODWELL,

THE FIRST

SCIENCE-MASTER APPOINTED AT MARLBOROUGH COLLEGE,

𝕿𝖍𝖎𝖘 𝕭𝖔𝖔𝖐 𝖎𝖘 𝕯𝖊𝖉𝖎𝖈𝖆𝖙𝖊𝖉

BY THE AUTHOR

AS A TOKEN OF ESTEEM AND GRATITUDE,

AND IN THE HOPE THAT

IT MAY EXCITE IN A FEW YOUNG PEOPLE SOME SMALL

FRACTION OF THE INTEREST AND ENTHUSIASM WHICH

HIS ADVENT AND HIS LECTURES AWAKENED

IN THE AUTHOR, UPON WHOM THE LIGHT

OF SCIENCE THEN SHONE FOR

THE FIRST TIME.

PREFACE.

I WOULD ask those readers who have grown up, and who may be disposed to find fault with this book, on the ground that in so many points it is incomplete, or that much is so elementary or well known, to remember that the lectures were meant for juveniles, and for juveniles only. These latter I would urge to do their best to repeat the experiments described. They will find that in many cases no apparatus beyond a few pieces of glass or india-rubber pipe, or other simple things easily obtained are required. If they will take this trouble they will find themselves well repaid, and if instead of being discouraged by a few failures they will persevere with the best means at their disposal, they will soon find more to interest them in experiments in which they only succeed after a little trouble than in those

which go all right at once. Some are so
simple that no help can be wanted, while some
will probably be too difficult, even with assist-
ance; but to encourage those who wish to see
for themselves the experiments that I have
described, I have given such hints at the end
of the book as I thought would be most
useful.

I have freely made use of the published
work of many distinguished men, among
whom I may mention Savart, Plateau, Clerk
Maxwell, Sir William Thomson, Lord Rayleigh, Mr. Chichester Bell, and Prof. Rücker.
The experiments have mostly been described
by them, some have been taken from journals,
and I have devised or arranged a few. I am
also indebted to Prof. Rücker for the use of
various pieces of apparatus which had been
prepared for his lectures.

SOAP-BUBBLES,

AND THE

FORCES WHICH MOULD THEM.

I DO not suppose that there is any one in this room who has not occasionally blown a common soap-bubble, and while admiring the perfection of its form, and the marvellous brilliancy of its colours, wondered how it is that such a magnificent object can be so easily produced.

I hope that none of you are yet tired of playing with bubbles, because, as I hope we shall see during the week, there is more in a common bubble than those who have only played with them generally imagine.

The wonder and admiration so beautifully portrayed by Millais in a picture, copies of which, thanks to modern advertising enterprise, some of you may possibly have seen, will, I hope, in no way fall away in consequence of these lectures; I think you will find that it will grow as your knowledge of the subject increases. You may be interested to hear that we are not the only juveniles who have played with bubbles. Ages ago children did the same, and though no mention of this is made by any of the classical authors, we know that they did, because there is an Etruscan vase in the Louvre in Paris of the greatest antiquity, on which children are represented blowing bubbles with a pipe. There is however, no means of telling now whose soap they used.

It is possible that some of you may like to know why I have chosen soap-bubbles as my subject; if so, I am glad to tell you. Though there are many subjects which might seem to a beginner to be more wonderful, more brilliant, or more exciting, there are few which so directly bear upon the things which we see every day. You cannot pour water from a jug or tea from a tea-pot; you cannot even do anything with a liquid of any kind, without setting in action the forces to which I am about to direct your attention. You cannot then fail to be frequently reminded of what you will hear and see in this room, and, what is perhaps most important of all, many of the things I am going to show you are so simple that you will be able without any apparatus to repeat for yourselves the experiments which I have prepared, and this you will find more interesting and instructive than merely listening to me and watching what I do.

There is one more thing I should like to explain, and that is why I am going to show experiments at all. You will at once answer because it would be so dreadfully dull if I didn't. Perhaps it would. But that is not the only reason. I would remind you then that when we want to find out anything that we do not know, there are two ways of proceeding. We may either ask somebody else who does know, or read what the most learned men have written about it, which is a very good plan if anybody happens to be able to answer our question; or else we may adopt the other plan, and by arranging an experiment, try for ourselves. An experiment is a question

which we ask of Nature, who is always ready
to give a correct answer, provided we ask
properly, that is, provided we arrange a proper
experiment. An experiment is not a conjuring
trick, something simply to make you wonder,
nor is it simply shown because it is beautiful,
or because it serves to relieve the monotony
of a lecture; if any of the experiments I show
are beautiful, or do serve to make these lectures a little less dull, so much the better;
but their chief object is to enable you to see
for yourselves what the true answers are to
questions that I shall ask.

Now I shall begin by performing an experiment which you have all probably tried dozens
of times. I have in my hand a common
camel's-hair brush. If you want to make the
hairs cling together and come to a point, you
wet it, and then you say the hairs cling together because the brush is wet. Now let us
try the experiment; but as you cannot see
this brush across the room, I hold it in front
of the lantern, and you can see it enlarged
upon the screen (Fig. 1, left hand). Now it
is dry, and the hairs are separately visible. I
am now dipping it in the water, as you can

see, and on taking it out, the hairs, as we expected, cling together (Fig. 1, right hand), because they are wet, as we are in the habit of saying. I shall now hold the brush in the water, but there it is evident that the

Fig. 1.

hairs do not cling at all (Fig. 1, middle), and yet they surely are wet now, being actually in the water. It would appear then that the reason which we always give is not exactly correct. This experiment, which requires nothing more than a brush and a glass of

water, then shows that the hairs of a brush
cling together not only because they are
wet, but for some other reason as well
which we do not yet know. It also shows
that a very common belief as to opening our
eyes under water is not founded on fact. It
is very commonly said that if you dive into
the water with your eyes shut you cannot see
properly when you open them under water,
because the water gums the eyelashes down
over the eyes; and therefore you must dive in
with your eyes open if you wish to see under
water. Now as a matter of fact this is not
the case at all; it makes no difference whether
your eyes are open or not when you dive in,
you can open them and see just as well either
way. In the case of the brush we have seen
that water does not cause the hairs to cling
together or to anything else when under the
water, it is only when taken out that this is
the case. This experiment, though it has not
explained why the hairs cling together, has at
any rate told us that the reason always given
is not sufficient.

I shall now try another experiment as simple
as the last. I have a pipe from which water

is very slowly issuing, but it does not fall away continuously; a drop forms which slowly grows until it has attained a certain definite size, and then it suddenly falls away. I want you to notice that every time this happens the drop is always exactly the same size and shape. Now this cannot be mere chance; there must be some reason for the definite size, and shape. Why does the water remain at all? It is heavy and is ready to fall, but it does not fall; it remains clinging until it is a certain size, and then it suddenly breaks away, as if whatever held it was not strong enough to carry a greater weight. Mr. Worthington has carefully drawn on a magnified scale the exact shape of a drop of water of different sizes, and these you now see upon the diagram on the wall (Fig. 2). These diagrams will probably suggest the idea that the water is hanging suspended in an elastic bag, and that the bag breaks or is torn away when there is too great a weight for it to carry. It is true there is no bag at all really, but yet the drops take a shape which suggests an elastic bag. To show you that this is no fancy, I have supported by a tripod a large

ring of wood over which a thin sheet of india-
rubber has been stretched, and now on allowing
water to pour in from this pipe you will see the
rubber slowly stretching under the increasing
weight, and, what I especially want you to

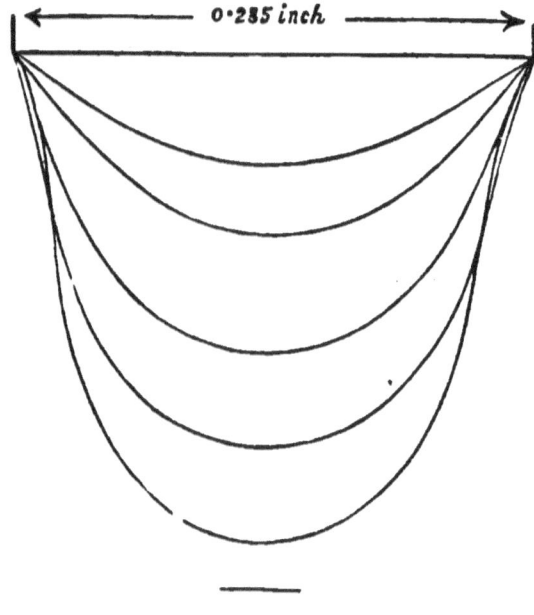

Fig. 2.

notice, it always assumes a form like those on
the diagram.   As the weight of water increases
the bag stretches, and now that there is about
a pailful of water in it, it is getting to a
state which indicates that it cannot last much
longer; it is like the water-drop just before

it falls away, and now suddenly it changes its shape (Fig. 3), and it would immediately tear

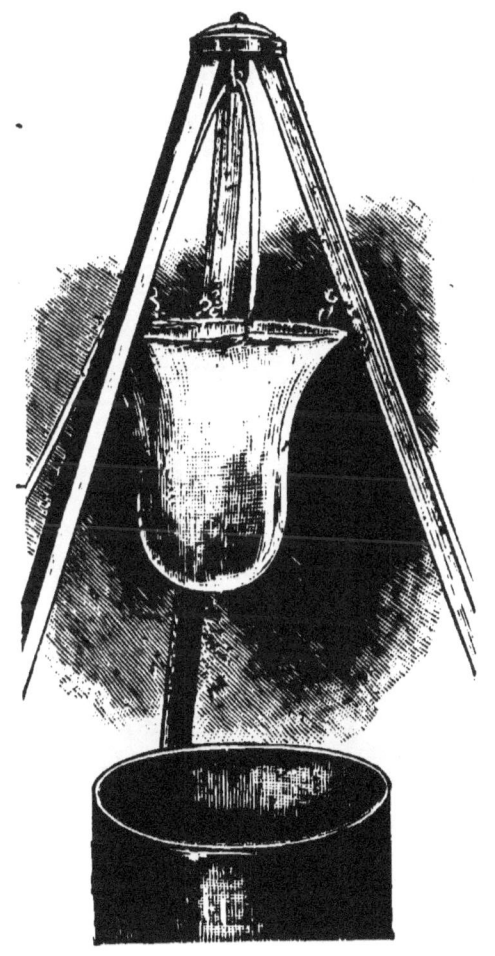

Fig. 3.

itself away if it were not for the fact that india-rubber does not stretch indefinitely; after a time it gets tight and will withstand a greater

B

pull without giving way. You therefore see the great drop now permanently hanging which is almost exactly the same in shape as the water-drop at the point of rupture. I shall now let the water run out by means of a syphon, and then the drop slowly contracts again. Now in this case we clearly have a heavy liquid in an elastic bag, whereas in the drop of water we have the same liquid but no bag that is visible. As the two drops behave in almost exactly the same way, we should naturally be led to expect that their form and movements are due to the same cause, and that the small water-drop has something holding it together like the india-rubber you now see.

Let us see how this fits the first experiment with the brush. That showed that the hairs do not cling together simply because they are wet; it is necessary also that the brush should be taken out of the water, or in other words it is necessary that the surface or the skin of the water should be present to bind the hairs together. If then we suppose that the surface of water is like an elastic skin, then both the experiments with the wet brush and with the water-drop will be explained.

Let us therefore try another experiment to see whether in other ways water behaves as if it had an elastic skin.

I have here a plain wire frame fixed to a stem with a weight at the bottom, and a hollow glass globe fastened to it with sealing-wax. The globe is large enough to make the whole thing float in water with the frame up in the air. I can of course press it down so that the frame touches the water. To make the movement of the frame more evident there is fixed to it a paper flag.

Now if water behaves as if the surface were an elastic skin, then it should resist the upward passage of the frame which I am now holding below the surface. I let go, and instead of bobbing up as it would do if there were no such action, it remains tethered down by this skin of the water. If I disturb the water so as to let the frame out at one corner, then, as you see, it dances up immediately (Fig. 4). You can see that the skin of the water must have been fairly strong, because a weight of about one quarter of an ounce placed upon the frame is only just sufficient to make the whole thing sink.

This apparatus which was originally described

by Van der Mensbrugghe I shall make use of
again in a few minutes.

I can show you in a more striking way that
there is this elastic layer or skin on pure clean
water. I have a small sieve made of wire
gauze sufficiently coarse to
allow a common pin to be
put through any of the
holes. There are moreover
about eleven thousand of
these holes in the bottom
of the sieve. Now, as you
know, clean wire is wetted
by water, that is, if it is
dipped in water it comes
out wet; on the other hand,
some materials, such as
paraffin wax, of which
paraffin candles are made,
are not wetted or really
touched by water, as you
may see for yourselves if you will only dip a
paraffin candle into water. I have melted a
quantity of paraffin in a dish and dipped this
gauze into the melted paraffin so as to coat
the wire all over with it, but I have shaken

Fig. 4.

it well while hot to knock the paraffin out of
the holes. ·You can now see on the screen that
the holes, all except one or two, are open, and
that a common pin can be passed through
readily enough. This then is the apparatus.
Now if water has an elastic skin which it requires force to stretch, it ought not to run
through these holes very readily; it ought

not to be able to
get through at all
unless forced, be-
cause at each hole
the skin would
have to be stretch-
ed to allow the
water to get to the
other side. : This
you understand is

Fig. 5.

only true if the water does not wet or really
touch the wire. Now to prevent the water
that I am going to pour in from striking the
bottom with so much force as to drive it
through, I have laid a small piece of paper
in the sieve, and am pouring the water on to
the paper, which breaks the fall (Fig. 5). I
have now poured in about half a tumbler of

water, and I might put in more. I take away
the paper but not a drop runs through. If
I give the sieve a jolt then the water is driven
to the other side, and in a moment it has all
escaped. Perhaps this will remind you of
one of the exploits of our old friend Simple
Simon,

> "Who went for water in a sieve,
> But soon it all ran through."

But you see if you only manage the sieve
properly, this is not quite so absurd as people
generally suppose.

If now I shake the water off the sieve, I can,
for the same reason, set it to float on water,
because its weight is not sufficient to stretch
the skin of the water through all the holes.
The water, therefore, remains on the other side,
and it floats even though, as I have already
said, there are eleven thousand holes in the
bottom, any one of which is large enough to
allow an ordinary pin to pass through. This
experiment also illustrates how difficult it is to
write real and perfect nonsense.

You may remember one of the stories in
Lear's book of Nonsense Songs.

" They went to sea in a sieve, they did,
   In a sieve they went to sea :
   In spite of all their friends could say,
   On a winter's morn, on a stormy day,
   In a sieve they went to sea.
*   *   *   *
" They sailed away in a sieve, they did,
   In a sieve they sailed so fast,
   With only a beautiful pea-green veil,
   Tied with a riband by way of a sail,
   To a small tobacco-pipe mast ;
*   *   *   *

And so on. You see that it is quite possible to go to sea in
a sieve—that is, if
the sieve is large
enough and the water
is not too rough—and
that the above lines
are now realized in
every particular (Fig.
6).

I may give one more
example of the power
of this elastic skin of
water. If you wish
to pour water from a
tumbler into a narrow-

Fig. 6.

necked bottle, you know how if you pour
slowly it nearly all runs down the side of the
glass and gets spilled about, whereas if you
pour quickly there is no room for the great
quantity of water to pass into the bottle all at
once, and so it gets spilled again.   But if you
take a piece of stick or a glass rod, and hold it

against the edge of the
tumbler, then the water
runs down the rod and
into the bottle, and none
is lost (Fig. 7) ; you may
even hold the rod inclined
to one side, as I am now
doing, but the water runs
down the wet rod because
this elastic skin forms a
kind of tube which pre-
vents the water from escap-

Fig. 7.

ing.   This action is often made use of in the
country to carry the water from the gutters
under the roof into a water-butt below.   A
piece of stick does nearly as well as an iron
pipe, and it does not cost anything like so
much.

I think then I have now done enough to

show that on the surface of water there is a kind of elastic skin. I do not mean that there is anything that is not water on the surface, but that the water while there acts in a different way to what it does inside, and that it acts as if it were an elastic skin made of something like very thin india-rubber, only that it is perfectly and absolutely elastic, which india-rubber is not.

You will now be in a position to understand how it is that in narrow tubes water does not find its own level, but behaves in an unexpected manner.— I have placed in front of the lantern a dish of water coloured blue so that you may the more easily see it. I shall now dip into the water a very narrow glass pipe, and immediately the water rushes up and stands about half an inch above the general level. The tube inside is wet. The elastic skin of the water is therefore attached to the tube, and goes on pulling up the water until the weight of the water raised above the general level is equal to the force exerted by the skin. If I take a tube about twice as big, then this pulling action which is going on all round the tube will cause it to lift twice the weight of water, but this will not make the water rise twice as high, because the larger tube holds so much more water for a given length than the smaller tube. It will not even pull it up as high as it did in the case of the smaller tube, because if it were pulled up as high the weight of the water raised would in that case be four times as great, and not only twice as great, as you might at first think. It will therefore only raise the water in the larger tube to half the height, and now that the two tubes are side by side you see the water in the smaller tube standing twice as high as it does in the larger tube. In the same way, if I were to take a tube as fine as a hair the water would go up ever so much higher. It is for this reason that this is called Capillarity, from the Latin word *capillus*, a hair, because the action is so marked in a tube the size of a hair.

Supposing now you had a great number of tubes of all sizes, and placed them in a row with the smallest on one side and all the others in the order of their sizes, then it is evident that the water would rise highest in the smallest tube and less and less high in each tube in the row (Fig. 8), until when you came to a very large tube you would not be able to see that the water was raised at all. You can very

easily obtain the same kind of effect by simply
taking two square pieces of window glass and
placing them face to face with a common
match or small fragment of anything to keep
them a small distance apart along one edge

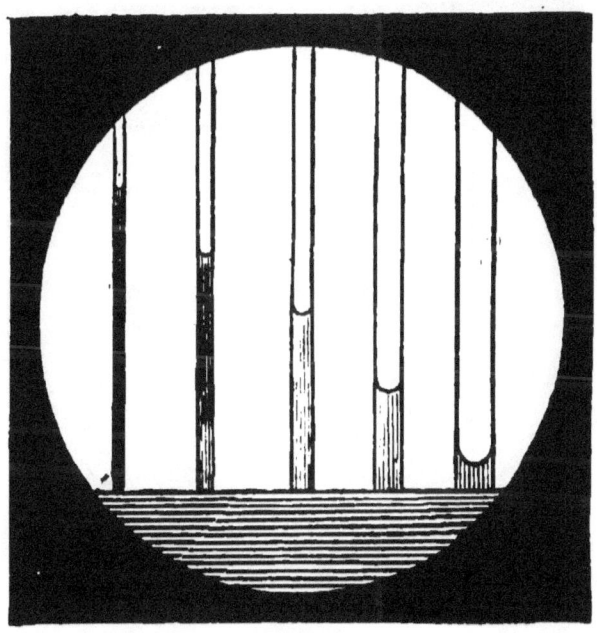

Fig. 8.

while they meet together along the opposite
edge. An india-rubber ring stretched over
them will hold them in this position. I now
take this pair of plates and stand it in a dish of
coloured water, and you at once see that the
water creeps up to the top of the plates on

the edge where they meet, and as the distance
between the plates gradually increases, so the
height to which the water rises gradually gets
less, and the result is that the surface of the
liquid forms a beautifully regular curve which

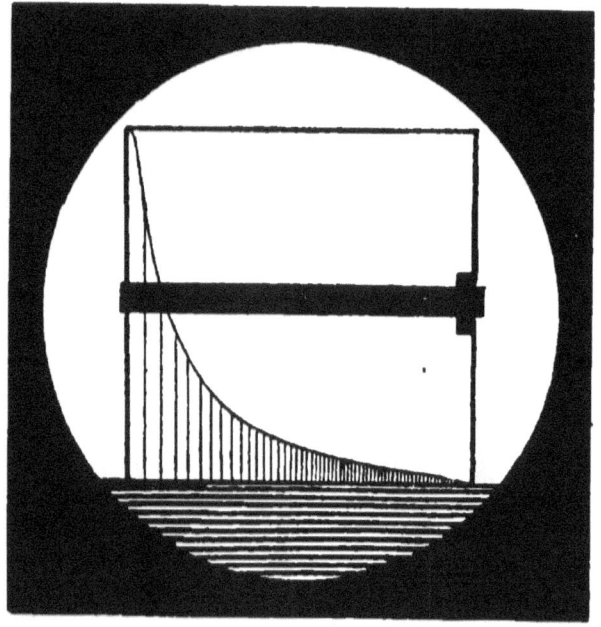

Fig. 9.

is called by mathematicians a rectangular
hyperbola (Fig. 9). I shall have presently
to say more about this and some other curves,
and so I shall not do more now than state
that the hyperbola is formed because as the
width between the plates gets greater the

height gets less, or, what comes to the same thing, because the weight of liquid pulled up at any small part of the curve is always the same.

If the plates or the tubes had been made of material not wetted by water, then the effect of the tension of the surface would be to drag the liquid away from the narrow spaces, and the more so as the spaces were narrower. As it is not easy to show this well with paraffined glass plates or tubes and water, I shall use another liquid which does not wet or touch clean glass, namely, quicksilver. As it is not possible to see through quicksilver, it will not do to put a narrow tube into this liquid to show that the level is lower in the tube than in the surrounding vessel, but the same result may be obtained by having a wide and a narrow tube joined together. Then, as you see upon the screen, the quicksilver is lower in the narrow than in the wide tube, whereas in a similar apparatus the reverse is the case with water (Fig. 10).

I want you now to consider what is happening when two flat plates partly immersed in water are held close together. We have seen that the water rises between them. Those parts of these two plates, which have air between them and also air outside them (indicated by the letter *a* in Fig. 11), are each of them pressed equally in opposite directions by

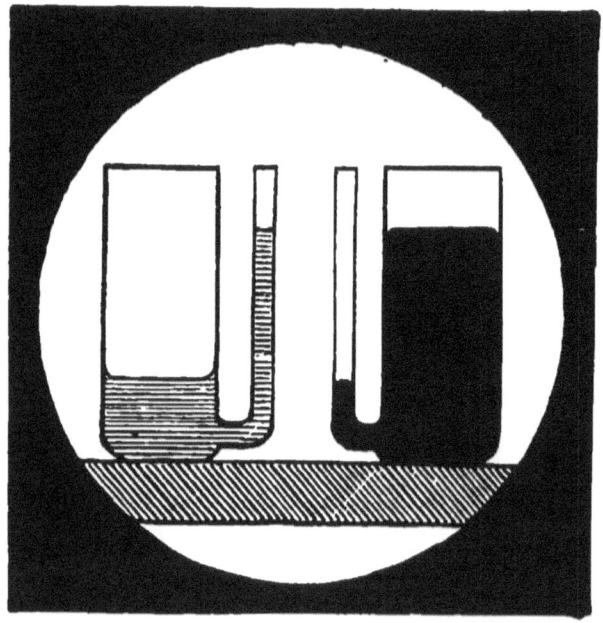

Fig. 10.

the pressure of the air, and so these parts do not tend to approach or to recede from one another. These parts again which have water on each side of each of them (as indicated by the letter *c*) are equally pressed in opposite directions by the pressure of the water, and so these parts do not tend to approach or to recede from one another.   But those parts of the plates (*b*) which have water between them and air outside would, you might think, be pushed apart by the water between them with a greater force than that which could be exerted by the air outside, and so you might

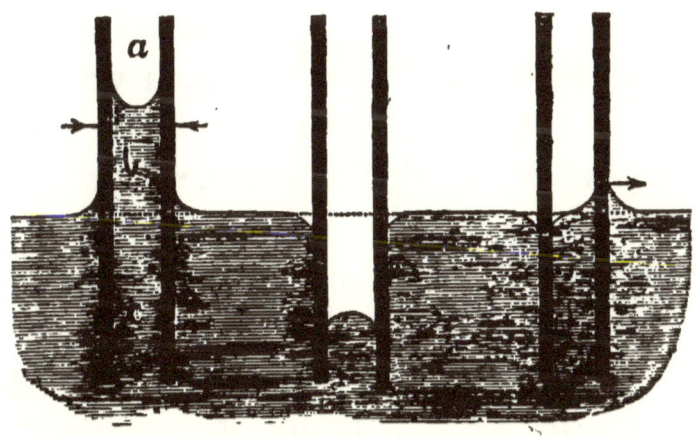

Fig. 11.

be led to expect that on this account a pair of plates if free to move would separate at once. But such an idea though very natural is wrong, and for this reason.   The water that is raised between the plates being above the general level must be under a less pressure, because, as every one knows, as you go down in water

the pressure increases, and so as you go up
the pressure must get less. The water then
that is raised between the plates is under a
less pressure than the air outside, and so on
the whole the plates are pushed together.
You can easily see that this is the case. I
have two very light hollow glass beads such
as are used to decorate a Christmas tree.
These will float in water if one end is stopped
with sealing-wax. These are both wetted by
water, and so the water between them is
slightly raised, for they act in the same way as
the two plates, but not so powerfully. However, you will have no difficulty in seeing that
the moment I leave them alone they rush
together with considerable force. Now if you
refer to the second figure in the diagram,
which represents two plates which are neither
of them wetted, I think you will see, without
any explanation from me, that they should be
pressed together, and this is made evident by
experiment. Two other beads which have been
dipped in paraffin wax so that they are neither
of them wetted by water float up to one another
again when separated as though they attracted
each other just as the clean glass beads did.

If you again consider these two cases, you will see that a plate that is wetted tends to move towards the higher level of the liquid, whereas one that is not wetted tends to move towards the lower level, that is if the level of the liquid on the two sides is made different by capillary action. Now suppose one plate wetted and the other not wetted, then, as the diagram imperfectly shows, the level of the liquid between the plates *where it meets* the non-wetted plate is higher than that outside, while where it meets the wetted plate it is lower than that outside; so each plate tends to go away from the other, as you can see now that I have one paraffined and one clean ball floating in the same water. They appear to repel one another.

You may also notice that the surface of the liquid near a wetted plate is curved, with the hollow of the curve upwards, while near a non-wetted plate the reverse is the case. That this curvature of the surface is of the first importance I can show you by a very simple experiment, which you can repeat at home as easily as the last that I have shown. I have a clean glass bead floating in water in a clean glass vessel, which is not quite full. The bead always goes to the side of the vessel. It is impossible to make it remain in the middle, it always gets to one side or the other directly. I shall now gradually add water until the level of the water is rather higher than that of the edge of the vessel. The surface is then rounded near the vessel, while it is hollow near the bead, and now the bead sails away towards the centre, and can by no possibility be made to stop near either side. With a paraffined bead the reverse is the case, as you would expect. Instead of a paraffined bead you may use a common needle, which you will find will float on water in a tumbler, if placed upon it very gently. If the tumbler is not quite full the needle will always go away from the edge, but if rather over-filled it will work up to one side, and then possibly roll over the edge; any bubbles, on the other hand, which were adhering to the glass before will, the instant that the water is above the edge of the glass, shoot away from the edge in the most sudden and surprising manner. This sudden change can be most easily seen by nearly filling the glass with water, and then gradually dipping in and taking out a cork, which will cause the level to slowly change.

So far I have given you no idea what force is exerted by this elastic skin of water. Measurements made with narrow tubes, with drops, and in other ways, all show that it is almost exactly equal to the weight of three and a quarter grains to the inch. We have, moreover, not yet seen whether other liquids act in the same way, and if so whether in other cases the strength of the elastic skin is the same.

You now see a second tube identical with that from which drops of water were formed, but in this case the liquid is alcohol. Now that drops are forming, you see at once that while alcohol makes drops which have a definite size and shape when they fall away, the alcohol drops are not by any means so large as the drops of water which are falling by their side. Two possible reasons might be given to explain this. Either alcohol is a heavier liquid than water, which would account for the smaller drop if the skin in each liquid had the same strength, or else if alcohol is not heavier than water its skin must be weaker than the skin of water. As a matter of fact alcohol is a lighter liquid than water, and so still more must the skin of alcohol be weaker than that of water.

We can easily put this to the test of experiment. In the game that is called the tug-of-war you know well enough which side is the strongest; it is the side which pulls the other over the line. Let us then make alcohol and

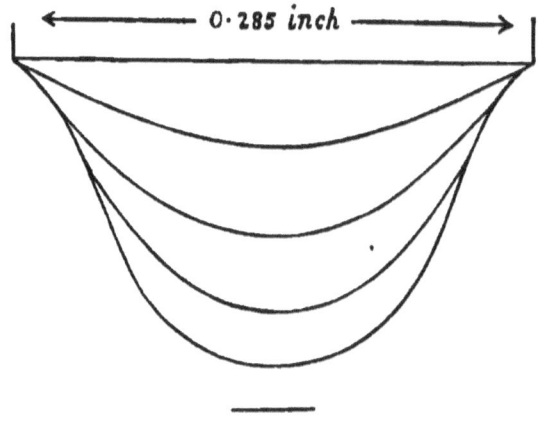

Fig. 12.

water play the same game. In order that you may see the water, it is coloured blue. It is lying as a shallow layer on the bottom of this white dish. At the present time the skin of the water is pulling equally in all directions, and so nothing happens; but if I pour a few drops of alcohol into the middle, then at the line which separates the alcohol from the water

we have alcohol on one side pulling in, while
we have water on the other side pulling out,
and you see the result. The water is victori-
ous; it rushes away in all directions, carrying a
quantity of the alcohol away with it, and leaves
the bottom of the dish dry (Fig. 13).

Fig. 13.

This difference in the strength of the skin
of alcohol and of water, or of water containing
much or little alcohol, gives rise to a curious
motion which you may see on the side of a
wine-glass in which there is some fairly strong
wine, such as port. The liquid is observed to

climb up the sides of the glass, then to gather into drops, and to run down again, and this goes on for a long time. This is explained as follows:—The thin layer of wine on the side of the glass being exposed to the air, loses its alcohol by evaporation more quickly than the wine in the glass. It therefore becomes weaker in alcohol or stronger in water than that below, and for this reason it has a stronger skin. It therefore pulls up more wine from below, and this goes on until there is so much that drops form, and it runs back again into the glass, as you now see upon the screen (Fig. 14). There can be no doubt that this movement is referred to in Proverbs xxiii. 31 : "Look not thou upon the wine when it is red, when it giveth his colour in the cup, when it moveth itself aright."

If you remember that this movement only occurs with strong wine, and that it must have been known to every one at the time that these words were written, and used as a test of the strength of wine, because in those days every one drank wine, then you will agree that this explanation of the meaning of that verse is the right one. I would ask you also to consider

whether it is not probable that other passages
which do not now seem to convey to us any
meaning whatever, may not in the same way
have referred to the common knowledge and

Fig. 14.

customs of the day, of which at the present
time we happen to be ignorant.

Ether, in the same way, has a skin which
is weaker than the skin of water. The very
smallest quantity of ether on the surface of
water will produce a perceptible effect. For
instance, the wire frame which I left some

time ago is still resting against the water-skin. The buoyancy of the glass bulb is trying to push it through, but the upward force is just not sufficient. I will however pour a few drops of ether into a glass, and simply pour the vapour upon the surface of the water (not a drop of *liquid* is passing over), and almost immediately sufficient ether has condensed upon the water to reduce the strength of the skin to such an extent that the frame jumps up out of the water.

There is a well-known case in which the difference between the strength of the skins of two liquids may be either a source of vexation or, if we know how to make use of it, an advantage. If you spill grease on your coat you can take it out very well with benzine. Now if you apply benzine to the grease, and then apply fresh benzine to that already there, you have this result—there is then greasy benzine on the coat to which you apply fresh benzine. It so happens that greasy benzine has a stronger skin than pure benzine. The greasy benzine therefore plays at tug-of-war with pure benzine, and being stronger wins and runs away in all directions, and the more you apply benzine the more the greasy benzine runs away carrying the grease with it. But if you follow the directions on the bottle, and first make a ring of clean benzine round the grease-spot, and then apply benzine to the grease, you then have the greasy benzine running away from the pure benzine ring and heaping itself together in the middle, and escaping into the fresh rag that you apply, so that the grease is all of it removed.

There is a difference again between hot and cold grease, as you may see, when you get home, if you watch a common candle burning. Close to the flame the grease is hotter than it is near the outside. It has therefore a weaker skin, and so a perpetual circulation is kept up, and the grease runs out on the surface and back again below, carrying little specks of dust which make this movement visible, and making the candle burn regularly.

You probably know how to take out grease-stains with a hot poker and blotting-paper. Here again the same kind of action is going on.

A piece of lighted camphor floating in water is another example of movement set up by

differences in the strength of the skin of water
owing to the action of the camphor.

I will give only one more example.

If you are painting in water-colours on
greasy paper or certain shiny surfaces the paint
will not lie smoothly on the paper, but runs
together in the well-known way; a very little
ox-gall, however, makes it lie perfectly, because
ox-gall so reduces the strength of the skin of
water that it will wet surfaces that pure water
will not wet. This reduction of the surface
tension you can see if I use the same wire
frame a third time. The ether has now
evaporated, and I can again make it rest against
the surface of the water, but very soon after I
touch the water with a brush containing ox-gall
the frame jumps up as suddenly as before.

It is quite unnecessary that I should any
further insist upon the fact that the outside of
a liquid acts as if it were a perfectly elastic
skin stretched with a certain definite force.

Suppose now that you take a small quantity
of water, say as much as would go into a nut-
shell, and suddenly let it go, what will happen?
Of course it will fall down and be dashed
against the ground. Or again, suppose you

take the same quantity of water and lay it carefully upon a cake of paraffin wax dusted over with lycopodium which it does not wet, what will happen? Here again the weight of the drop—that which makes it fall if not held —will squeeze it against the paraffin and make it spread out into a flat cake. What would happen if the weight of the drop or the force pulling it downwards could be prevented from acting?. In such a case the drop would only feel the effect of the elastic skin, which would try to pull it into such a form as to make the surface as small as possible. It would in fact rapidly become a perfectly round ball, because in no other way can so small a surface be obtained. If, instead of taking so much water, we were to take a drop about as large as a pin's head, then the weight which tends to squeeze it out or make it fall would be far less, while the skin would be just as strong, and would in reality have a greater moulding power, though why I cannot now explain. We should therefore expect that by taking a sufficiently small quantity of water the moulding power of the skin would ultimately be able almost entirely to counteract the weight of the drop, so that very small drops should appear like perfect little balls. If you have found any difficulty in following this argument, a very simple illustration will make it clear. You many of you probably know how by folding paper to make this little thing which I hold in my hand (Fig. 15). It is called a cat-box, because of its power of dispelling cats when it is filled

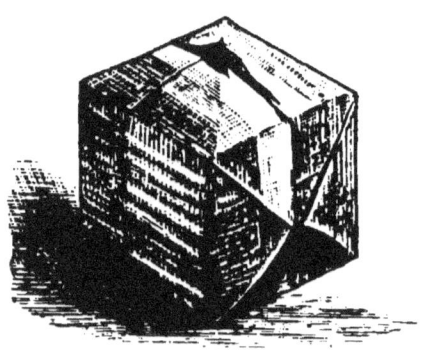

Fig. 15.

with water and well thrown. This one, large enough to hold about half a pint, is made out of a small piece of the *Times* newspaper. You may fill it with water and carry it about and throw it with your full power, and the strength of the paper skin is sufficient to hold it together until it hits anything, when of course it bursts and the water comes out. On the other hand, the large one made out of a whole sheet of the *Times* is barely able to withstand the weight of the water that it will hold. It is only just strong enough to allow of its being filled and carried, and then it may be dropped from a height, but you cannot throw it. In the same way the weaker skin of a liquid will not make a large quantity take the shape of a ball, but it will mould a minute drop so perfectly that you cannot tell by looking at it that it is not perfectly round every way. This is most easily seen with quicksilver. A large quantity rolls about like a flat cake, but the very small drops obtained by throwing some violently on the table and so breaking it up appear perfectly round. You can see the same difference in the beads of gold now upon the screen (Fig. 16). They are now solid, but they were melted and then allowed to cool without being disturbed. Though the large bead is flattened by its weight, the small one appears perfectly round. Finally, you may see the same thing with water if you dust a little lycopodium on the table. Then water falling will roll itself up into perfect little balls. You may even see the same thing on a dusty day if you water the road with a water-pot.

If it were not for the weight of liquids, that is the force with which they are pulled down towards the earth, large drops would be as

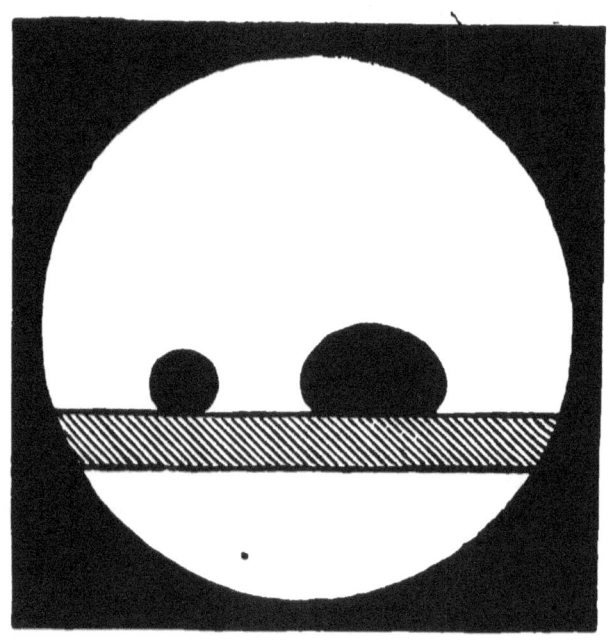

Fig. 16.

perfectly round as small ones. This was first beautifully shown by Plateau, the blind experimentalist, who placed one liquid inside another which is equally heavy, and with which it does not mix. Alcohol is lighter than oil, while water is heavier, but a suitable mixture of alcohol

and water is just as heavy as oil, and so oil does
not either tend to rise or to fall when immersed
in such a mixture. I have in front of the
lantern a glass box containing alcohol and
water, and by means of a tube I shall slowly
allow oil to flow in. You see that as I remove
the tube it becomes a perfect ball as large as a
walnut. There are now two or three of these
balls of oil all perfectly round. I want you to
notice that when I hit them on one side the
large balls recover their shape slowly, while the
small ones become round again much more
quickly. There is a very beautiful effect which
can be produced with this apparatus, and though
it is not necessary to refer to it, it is well
worth while now that the apparatus is set up
to show it to you. In the middle of the box
there is an axle with a disc upon it to which I
can make the oil adhere. Now if I slowly turn
the wire and disc the oil will turn also. As I
gradually increase the speed the oil tends to fly
away in all directions, but the elastic skin
retains it. The result is that the ball becomes
flattened at its poles like the earth itself. On
increasing the speed, the tendency of the oil to
get away is at last too much for the elastic skin,

and a ring breaks away (Fig. 17), which almost
immediately contracts again on to the rest of
the ball as the speed falls.   If I turn it sufficiently fast the ring breaks up into a series of
balls which you now see.   One cannot help

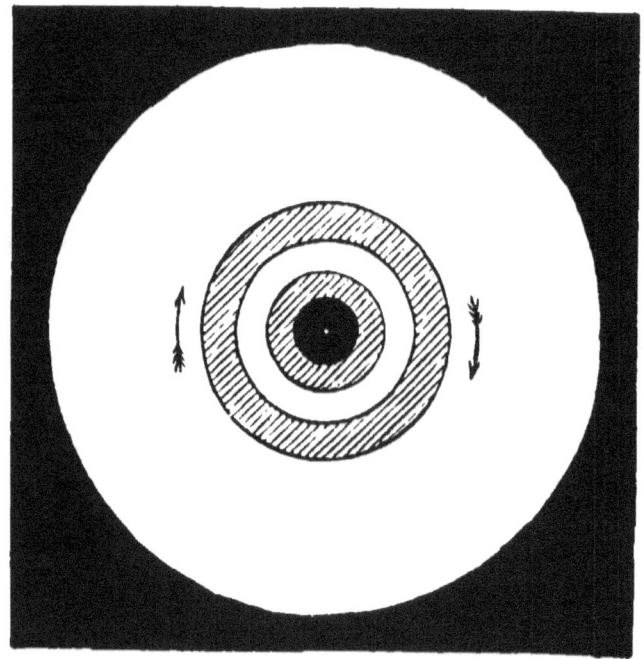

Fig. 17.

being reminded of the heavenly bodies by this
beautiful experiment of Plateau's, for you see a
central body and a series of balls of different
sizes all travelling round in the same direction
(Fig. 18); but the forces which are acting in

the two cases are totally distinct, and what you see has nothing whatever to do with the sun and the planets.

We have thus seen that a large ball of liquid can be moulded by the elasticity of its skin if

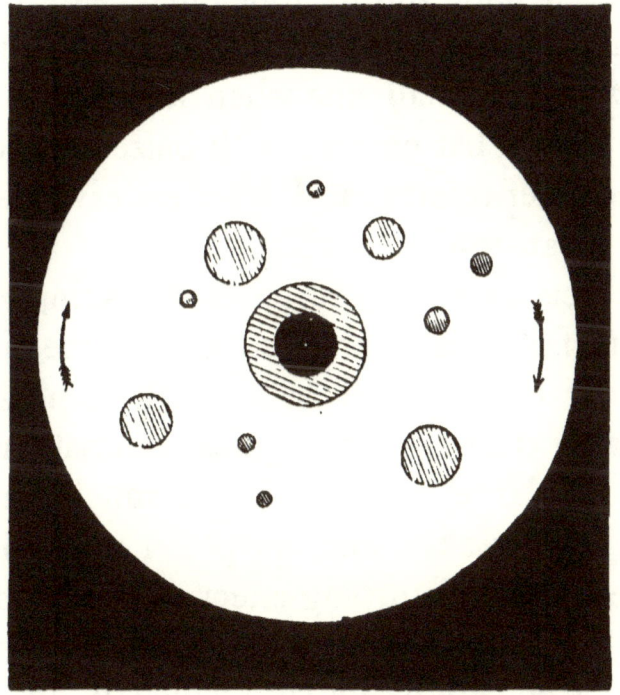

Fig. 18.

the disturbing effect of its weight is neutralized, as in the last experiment. This disturbing effect is practically of no account in the case of a soap-bubble, because it is so thin that it hardly weighs anything. You all know, of

D

course, that a soap-bubble is perfectly round, and now you know why; it is because the elastic film, trying to become as small as it can, must take the form which has the smallest surface for its content, and that form is the sphere. I want you to notice here, as with the oil, that a large bubble oscillates much more slowly than a small one when knocked out of shape with a·bat covered with baize or wool.

The chief result that I have endeavoured to make clear to-day is this. The outside of a liquid acts as if it were an elastic skin, which will, as far as it is able, so mould the liquid within it that it shall be as small as possible. Generally the weight of liquids, especially when there is a large quantity, is too much for the feebly elastic skin, and its power may not be noticed. The disturbing effect of weight is got rid of by immersing one liquid in another which is equally heavy with which it does not mix, and it is hardly noticed when very small drops are examined, or when a bubble is blown, for in these cases the weight is almost nothing, while the elastic power of the skin is just as great as ever.

LECTURE II.

I DID not in the last lecture by any direct experiment show that a soap-film or bubble is really elastic, like a piece of stretched india-rubber.

A soap-bubble, consisting, as it does, of a thin layer of liquid, which must have of course both an inside and an outside surface or skin, must be elastic, and this is easily shown in many ways. Perhaps the easiest way is to tie a thread across a ring rather loosely, and then to dip the ring into soap water. On taking it out there is a film stretched over the ring, in which the thread moves about quite freely, as you can see upon the screen. But if I break the film on one side, then immediately the thread is pulled by the film on the other side as far as it can go, and it is now tight (Fig. 19). You will also notice that it is part of a perfect circle, because that form makes the

space on one side as great, and therefore on
the other side, where the film is, as small,
as possible.   Or again, in this second ring the
thread is double for a short distance in the
middle.   If I break the film between the

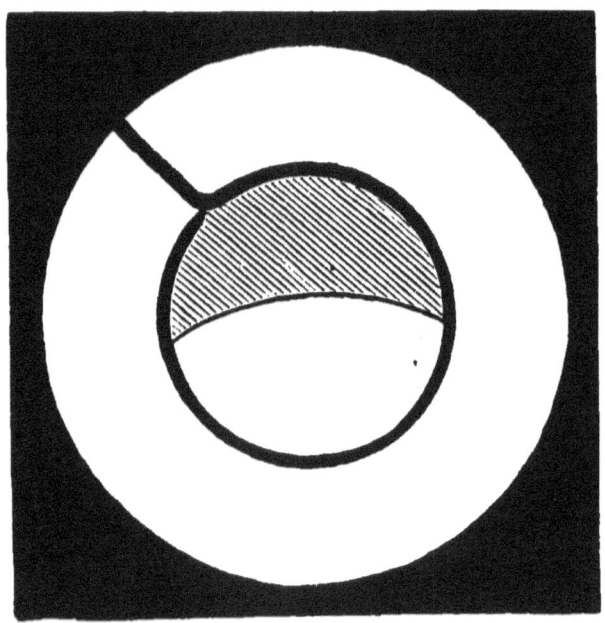

Fig. 19.

threads they are at once pulled apart, and are
pulled into a perfect circle (Fig. 20), because
that is the form which makes the space within
it as great as possible, and therefore leaves the
space outside it as small as possible.   You will
also notice, that though the circle will not

allow itself to be pulled out of shape, yet it can move about in the ring quite freely, because such a movement does not make any difference to the space outside it.

I have now blown a bubble upon a ring

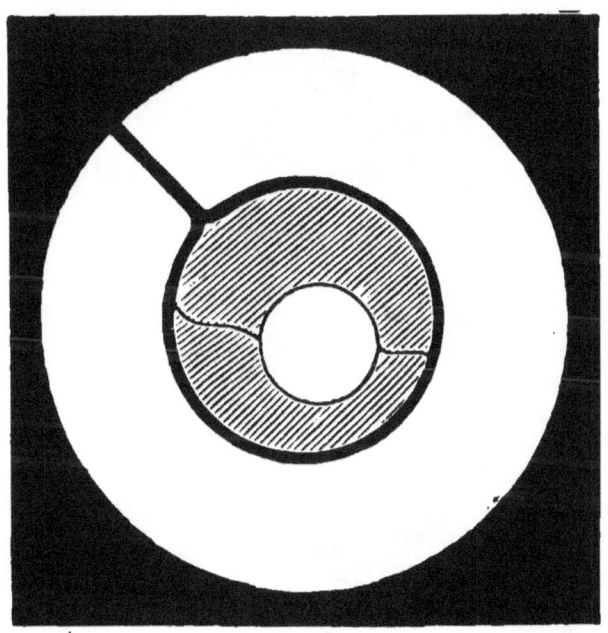

Fig. 20.

of wire. I shall hang a small ring upon it, and to show more clearly what is happening, I shall blow a little smoke into the bubble. Now that I have broken the film inside the lower ring, you will see the smoke being driven out and the ring lifted up, both of which show the elastic nature of the film. Or again, I have blown a bubble on the end of a wide pipe; on holding the open end of the pipe to a candle flame, the outrushing air blows out the flame at once, which shows that the soap-bubble is

Fig. 21.

acting like an elastic bag (Fig. 21). You now see that, owing to the elastic skin of a soap-bubble, the air inside is under pressure and will get out if it can. Which would you think would squeeze the air inside it most, a large or a small bubble? We will find out by

trying, and then see if we can tell why. You
now see two pipes each with a tap. These are
joined together by a third pipe in which there
is a third tap. I will first blow one bubble
and shut it off with the tap 1 (Fig. 22), and

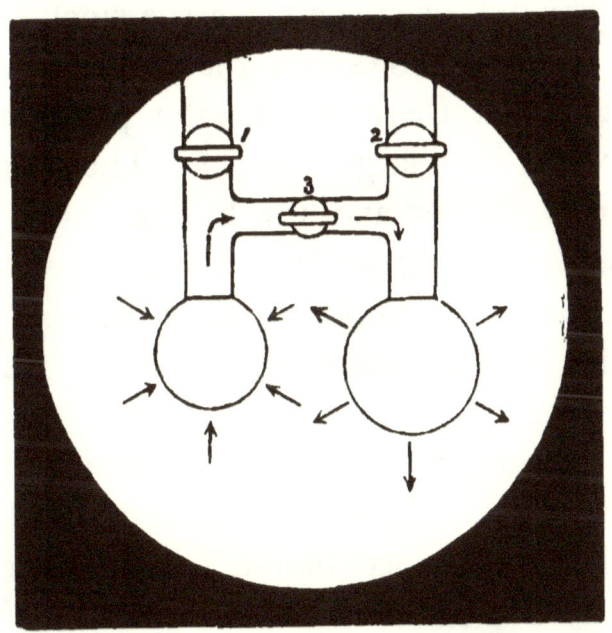

Fig. 22.

then the other, and shut it off with the tap 2.
They are now nearly equal in size, but the air
cannot yet pass from one to the other because
the tap 3 is turned off. Now if the pressure
in the largest one is greatest it will blow
air into the other when I open this tap,

until they are equal in size; if, on the other
hand, the pressure in the small one is greatest,
it will blow air into the large one, and will itself
get smaller until it has quite disappeared. We
will now try the experiment. You see immediately that I open the tap 3 the small bubble
shuts up and blows out the large one, thus
showing that there is a greater pressure in a
small than in a large bubble. The directions
in which the air and the bubble move is indicated in the figure by arrows. I want you
particularly to notice and remember this,
because this is an experiment on which a
great deal depends. To impress this upon
your memory I shall show the same thing in
another way. There is in front of the lantern
a little tube shaped like a U half filled with
water. One end of the U is joined to a pipe on
which a bubble can be blown (Fig. 23). You
will now be able to see how the pressure
changes as the bubble increases in size, because
the water will be displaced more when the pressure is more, and less when it is less. Now
that there is ɪ very small bubble, the pressure
as measured by the water is about one quarter
of an inch on the scale. The bubble is grow-

ing and the pressure indicated by the water in the gauge is falling, until, when the bubble is double its former size, the pressure is only half what it was; and this is always true, the

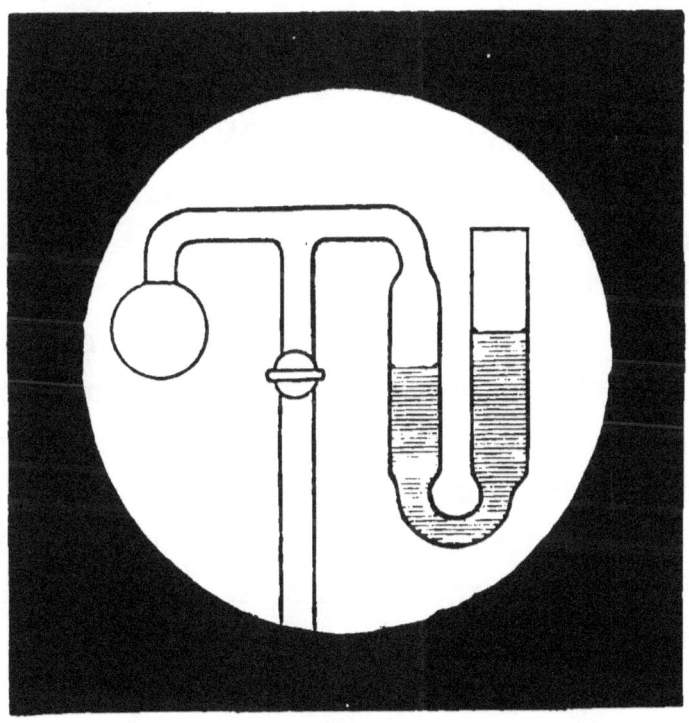

Fig. 23.

smaller the bubble the greater the pressure. As the film is always stretched with the same force, whatever size the bubble is, it is clear that the pressure inside can only depend upon the curvature of a bubble. In the case of lines, our ordinary language tells us, that the larger a circle is the less is its curvature; a piece of a small circle is said to be a quick or a sharp curve, while a piece of a great circle is only slightly curved; and if you take a piece of a very large circle indeed, then you cannot tell it from a straight line, and you say it is not curved at all. With a part of the surface of a ball it is just the same—the larger the ball the less it is curved; and if the ball is very large indeed, say 8000 miles across, you cannot tell a small piece of it from a true plane. Level water is part of such a surface, and you know that still water in a basin appears perfectly flat, though in a very large lake or the sea you can see that it is curved. We have seen that in large bubbles the pressure is little and the curvature is little, while in small bubbles the pressure is great and the curvature is great. The pressure and the curvature rise and fall together. We have now learnt the lesson which the experiment of the two bubbles, one blown out by the other, teaches us.

A ball or sphere is not the only form which you can give to a soap-bubble. If you take a bubble between two rings, you can pull it out until at last it has the shape of a round straight tube or cylinder as it is called. We have spoken of the curvature of a ball or sphere; now what is the curvature of a cylinder? Looked at sideways, the edge of the wooden cylinder upon the table appears straight, *i. e.* not curved at all; but looked at from above

Fig. 24.

it appears round, and is seen to have a definite curvature (Fig. 24). What then is the curvature of the surface of a cylinder? We have seen that the pressure in a bubble depends upon the curvature when they are spheres, and this is true whatever shape they have. If, then, we find what sized sphere will produce the same pressure upon the air inside that a cylinder does, then we shall know that the curvature of

the cylinder is the same as that of the sphere
which balances it. Now at each end of a
short tube I shall blow an ordinary bubble,
but I shall pull the lower bubble by means
of another tube into the cylindrical form, and
finally blow in more or less air until the sides

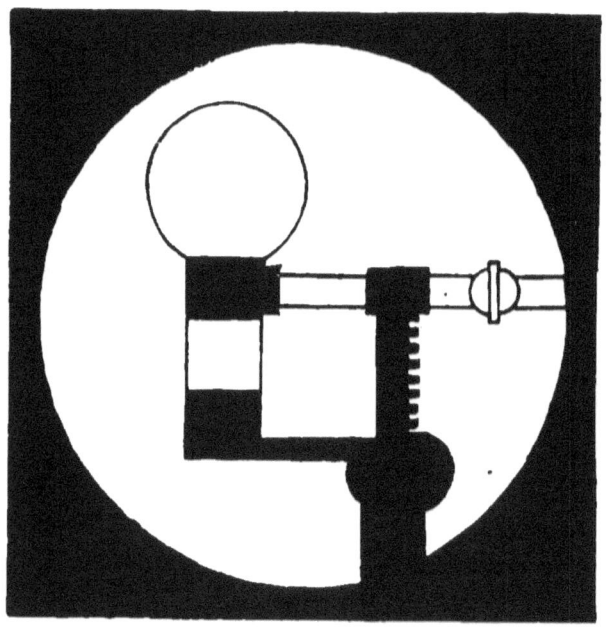

Fig. 25.

of the cylinder are perfectly straight. That is
now done (Fig. 25), and the pressure in the
two bubbles must be exactly the same, as there
is a free passage of air between the two. On
measuring them you see that the sphere is
exactly double the cylinder in diameter. But

this sphere has only half the curvature that a sphere half its diameter would have. Therefore the cylinder, which we know has the same curvature that the large sphere has, because the two balance, has only half the curvature of a sphere of its own diameter, and the pressure in it is only half that in a sphere of its own diameter.

I must now make one more step in explaining this question of curvature. Now that the cylinder and sphere are balanced I shall blow in more air, making the sphere larger; what will happen to the cylinder? The cylinder is, as you see, very short; will it become blown out too, or what will happen? Now that I am blowing in air you see the sphere enlarging, thus relieving the pressure; the cylinder develops a waist, it is no longer a cylinder, the sides are curved inwards. As I go on blowing and enlarging the sphere, they go on falling inwards, but not indefinitely. If I were to blow the upper bubble till it was of an enormous size the pressure would become extremely small. Let us make the pressure nothing at all at once by simply breaking the upper bubble, thus allowing the air a free passage from the inside to the outside of what was the cylinder. Let me repeat this experiment on a larger scale. I have two large glass rings, between which I can draw out a film of the

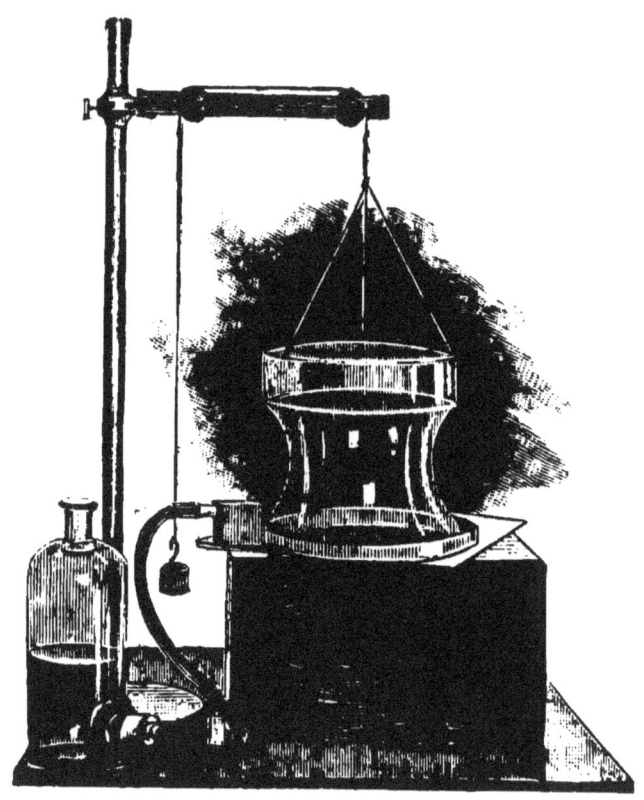

Fig. 26.

same kind. Not only is the outline of the soap-film curved inwards, but it is exactly the same as the smaller one in shape (Fig. 26). As there is now no pressure there ought to be no curvature, if what I have said is correct. But look at the soap-film. Who would venture to say that that was not curved? and yet we had satisfied ourselves that the pressure and the curvature rose and fell together. We now seem to have come to an absurd conclusion. Because the pressure is reduced to nothing we say the surface must have no curvature, and yet a glance is sufficient to show that the film is so far curved as to have a most elegant waist. Now look at the plaster model on the table, which is a model of a mathematical figure which also has a waist.

Let us therefore examine this cast more in detail. I have a disc of card which has exactly the same diameter as the waist of the cast. I now hold this edgeways against the waist (Fig. 27), and though you can see that it does not fit the whole curve, it fits the part close to the waist perfectly. This then shows that this part of the cast would appear curved inwards if you looked at it sideways, to the same extent that it would appear curved outwards if you could see it from above. So considering the waist only, it is curved both towards the inside and also away from the inside according to the way you look at it, and to the same extent. The curvature inwards would make the pressure inside less, and the curvature outwards would make it more, and as they are equal they just balance, and there is no pressure at all. If we could in the same way examine the

Fig. 27.

bubble with the waist, we should find that this was true not only at the waist but at every part of it. Any curved surface like this which at every point is equally curved opposite ways, is called a surface of no curvature, and so what seemed an absurdity is now explained. Now this surface, which is the only one of the kind

symmetrical about an axis, except a flat surface, is called a catenoid, because it is like a
chain, as you will see directly, and, as you
know, *catena* is the Latin for a chain. I shall
now hang a chain in a loop from a level stick,
and throw a strong light upon it, so that you
can see it well (Fig. 28). This is exactly the

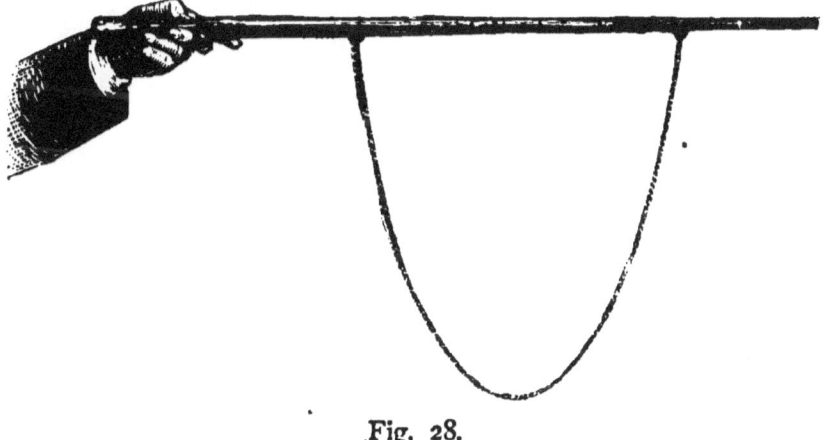

Fig. 28.

same shape as the side of a bubble drawn
out between two rings, and open at the end
to the air.[1]

Let us now take two rings, and having placed
a bubble between them, gradually alter the
pressure. You can tell what the pressure is

[1] If the reader finds these geometrical relations too
difficult to follow, he or she should skip the next pages,
and go on again at " We have found . . ." p. 77.

E

by looking at the part of the film which
covers either ring, which I shall call the cap.
This must be part of a sphere, and we know
that the curvature of this and the pressure
inside rise and fall together. I have now
adjusted the bubble so that it is a nearly

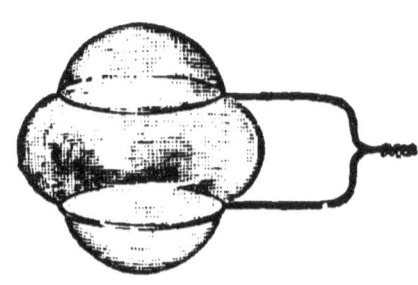

Fig. 29.

perfect sphere. If
I blow in more air
the caps become
more curved, show-
ing an increased
pressure, and the
sides bulge out even
more than those of

a sphere (Fig. 29). I have now brought the
whole bubble back to the spherical form. A
little increased pressure, as shown by the
increased curvature of the cap, makes the
sides bulge more; a little less pressure, as
shown by the flattening of the caps, makes
the sides bulge less. Now the sides are
straight, and the cap, as we have already
seen, forms part of a sphere of twice the
diameter of the cylinder. I am still further
reducing the pressure until the caps are plane,
that is, not curved at all. There is now no

pressure inside, and therefore the sides have, as we have already seen, taken the form of a hanging chain; and now, finally, the pressure inside is less than that outside, as you can see by the caps being drawn inwards, and the sides have even a smaller waist than the catenoid. We have now seen seven curves as we gradually reduced the pressure, namely—

1. Outside the sphere.
2. The sphere.
3. Between the sphere and the cylinder.
4. The cylinder.
5. Between the cylinder and the catenoid.
6. The catenoid.
7. Inside the catenoid.

Now I am not going to say much more about all these curves, but I must refer to the very curious properties that they possess. In the first place, they must all of them have the same curvature in every part as the portion of the sphere which forms the cap; in the second place, they must all be the curves of the least possible surface which can enclose the air and join the rings as well. And finally, since they pass insensibly from one to the other as the pressure gradually changes, though they are

distinct curves there must be some curious and
intimate relation between them. Tl ˙ though
it is a little difficult, I shall explain. If I were
to say that these curves are the roulettes of
the conic sections I suppose I should alarm
you, and at the same time explain nothing, so
I shall not put it in that way; but instead, I
shall show you a simple experiment which will
throw some light upon the subject, which you
can try for yourselves at home.

I have here a common bedroom candlestick
with a flat round base.   Hold the candlestick
exactly upright near to a white wall, then you
will see the shadow of the base on the wall
below, and the outline of the shadow is a
symmetrical curve, called a hyperbola. Gradually tilt the candle away from the wall, you
will then notice the sides of the shadow
gradually branch away less and less, and when
you have so far tilted the candle away from
the wall that the flame is exactly above the
edge of the base,—and you will know when
this is the case, because then the falling grease
will just fall on the edge of the candlestick and
splash on to the carpet,—I have it so now,—
the sides of the shadow near the floor will be

almost parallel (Fig. 30), and the shape of the shadow ill have become a curve, known as a parabola; and now when the candlestick is still more tilted, so that the grease misses the

Fig. 30.

base altogether and falls in a gentle stream upon the carpet, you will see that the sides of the shadow have curled round and met on the wall, and you now have a curve like an oval, except that the two ends are alike, and this is

called an ellipse. If you go on tilting the
candlestick, then when the candle is just
level, and the grease pouring away, the shadow
will be almost a circle; it would be an exact
circle if the flame did not flare up. Now
if you go on tilting the candle, until at last
the candlestick is upside down, the curves
already obtained will be reproduced in the
reverse order, but above instead of below you.

You may well ask what all this has to do
with a soap-bubble. You will see in a moment.
When you light a candle, the base of the
candlestick throws the space behind it into
darkness, and the form of this dark space,
which is everywhere round like the base, and
gets larger as you get further from the flame,
is a cone, like the wooden model on the table.
The shadow cast on the wall is of course the
part of the wall which is within this cone. It
is the same shape that you would find if you
were to cut a cone through with a saw, and
so these curves which I have shown you are
called conic sections. You can see some of
them already made in the wooden model on
the table. If you look at the diagram on the
wall (Fig. 31), you will see a complete cone at

first upright
(A),then being
gradually tilted
over into the
positions that
I have speci-
fied. The black
line in the
upper part of
the diagram
shows where
the cone is cut
through, and
the shaded area
below shows
the true shape
of these shad-
ows, or pieces
cut off, which
are called sec-
tions. Now in
each of these
sections there
are either one
or two points,
each of which

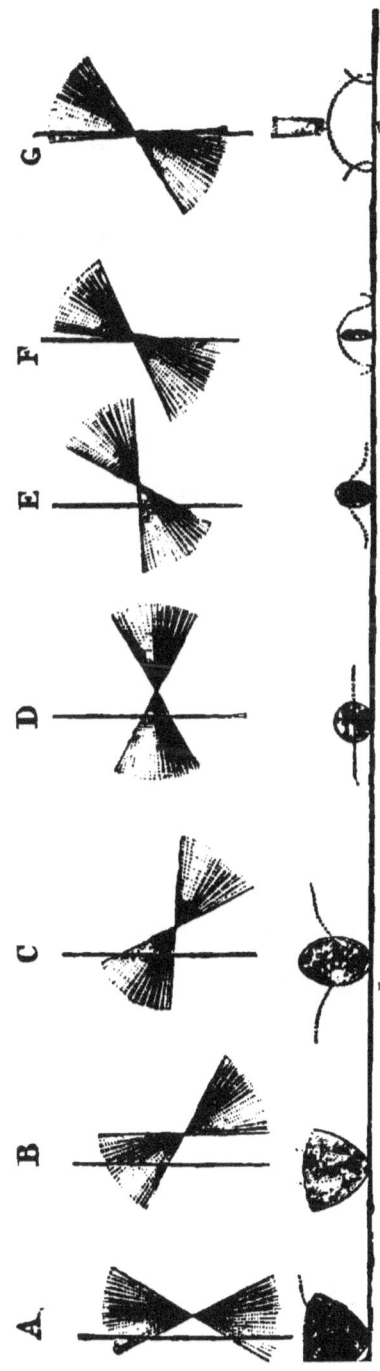

is called a focus, and these are indicated by
conspicuous dots. In the case of the circle
(D Fig. 31), this point is also the centre. Now
if this circle is made to roll like a wheel
along the straight line drawn just below it, a
pencil at the centre will rule the straight line
which is dotted in the lower part of the figure ;
but if we were to make wheels of the shapes of
any of the other sections, a pencil at the focus
would certainly not draw a straight line.
What shape it would draw is not at once
evident. First consider any of the elliptic
sections (C, E, or F) which you see on either
side of the circle. If these were wheels, and
were made to roll, the pencil as it moved along
would also move up and down, and the line it
would draw is shown dotted as before in the
lower part of the figure. In the same way the
other curves, if made to roll along a straight
line, would cause pencils at their focal points
to draw the other dotted lines.

We are now almost able to see what the
conic section has to do with a soap-bubble.
When a soap-bubble was blown between two
rings, and the pressure inside was varied, its
outline went through a series of forms, some

of which are represented by the dotted lines
in the lower part of the figure, but in every
case they could have been accurately drawn by
a pencil at the focus of a suitable conic section
made to roll on a straight line. I called one
of the bubble forms, if you remember, by its
name, catenoid; this is produced when there
is no pressure. The dotted curve in the second
figure B is this one; and to show that this
catenary can be so drawn, I shall roll upon a
straight edge a board made into the form of
the corresponding section, which is called a
parabola, and let the chalk at its focus draw
its curve upon the black board. There is
the curve, and it is as I said, exactly the curve
that a chain makes when hung by its two ends.
Now that a chain is so hung you see that it
exactly lies over the chalk line.

All this is rather difficult to understand,
but as these forms which a soap-bubble takes
afford a beautiful example of the most important principle of continuity, I thought it
would be a pity to pass it by. It may be put
in this way. A series of bubbles may be blown
between a pair of rings. If the pressures are
different the curves must be different. In

blowing them the pressures slowly and *continuously* change, and so the curves cannot be altogether different in kind. Though they may be different curves, they also must pass slowly and continuously one into the other. We find the bubble curves can be drawn by rolling wheels made in the shape of the conic sections on a straight line, and so the conic sections, though distinct curves, must pass slowly and continuously one into the other. This we saw was the case, because as the candle was slowly tilted the curves did as a fact slowly and insensibly change from one to the other. There was only one parabola, and that was formed when the side of the cone was parallel to the plane of section, that is when the falling grease just touched the edge of the candlestick; there is only one bubble with no pressure, the catenoid, and this is drawn by rolling the parabola. As the cone is gradually inclined more, so the sections become at first long ellipses, which gradually become more and more round until a circle is reached, after which they become more and more narrow until a line is reached. The corresponding bubble curves are produced by a gradually increasing pressure,

and, as the diagram shows, these bubble curves
are at first wavy (C), then they become straight
when a cylinder is formed (D), then they become wavy again (E and F), and at last, when
the cutting plane, *i. e.* the black line in the
upper figure, passes through the vertex of the
cone the waves become a series of semicircles,
indicating the ordinary spherical soap-bubble.
Now if the cone is inclined ever so little more a
new shape of section is seen (G), and this being
rolled, draws a curious curve with a loop in it;
but how this is so it would take too long to
explain. It would also take too long to trace
the further positions of the cone, and to trace
the corresponding sections and bubble curves
got by rolling them. Careful inspection of the
diagram may be sufficient to enable you to
work out for yourselves what will happen in all
cases. I should explain that the bubble surfaces are obtained by spinning the dotted lines
about the straight line in the lower part of
Fig. 31 as an axis.

As you will soon find out if you try, you
cannot make with a soap-bubble a great length
of any of these curves at one time, but you
may get pieces of any of them with no more

apparatus than a few wire rings, a pipe, and a little soap and water. You can even see the whole of one of the loops of the dotted curve of the first figure (A), which is called a nodoid, not a complete ring, for that is unstable, but a part of such a ring. Take a piece of wire or a match, and fasten one end to a piece of lead, so that it will stand upright in a dish of soap water, and project half an inch or so. Hold with one hand a sheet of glass resting on the match in middle, and blow a bubble in the water against the match. As soon as it touches the glass plate, which should be wetted with the soap solution, it will become a cylinder, which will meet the glass plate in a true circle. Now very slowly incline the plate. The bubble will at once work round to the lowest side, and try to pull itself away from the match stick, and in doing so it will develop a loop of the nodoid, which would be exactly true in form if the match or wire were slightly bent, so as to meet both the glass and the surface of the soap water at a right angle. I have described this in detail, because it is not generally known that a complete loop of the nodoid can be made with a soap-bubble.

We have found that the pressure in a short cylinder gets less if it begins to develop a waist, and greater if it begins to bulge. Let us therefore try and balance one with a bulge against another with a waist. Immediately that I open the tap and let the air pass, the one

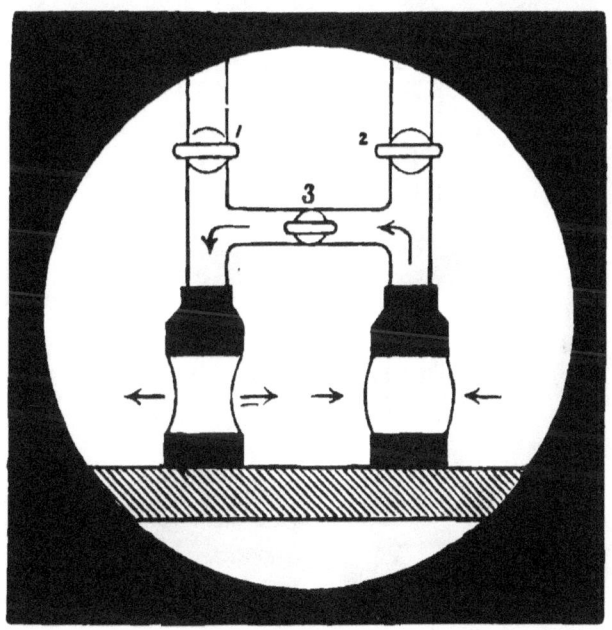

Fig. 32.

with a bulge blows air round to the one with a waist and they both become straight. In Fig. 32 the direction of the movement of the air and of the sides of the bubble is indicated by arrows. Let us next try the same experiment with a pair of rather longer cylinders, say about twice as long as they are wide. They are now ready, one with a bulge and one with a waist. Directly I open the tap, and let the air pass from one to the other, the one with

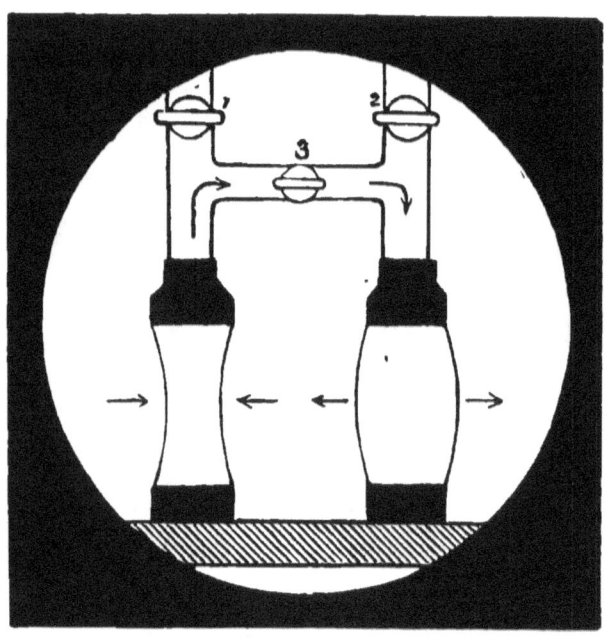

Fig. 33.

a waist blows out the other still more (Fig. 33), until at last it has shut itself up. It therefore behaves exactly in the opposite way that the short cylinder did. If you try pairs of cylinders of different lengths you will find that the change occurs when they are just over one

and a half times as long as they are wide.
Now if you imagine one of these tubes joined
on to the end of the other, you will see that a
cylinder more than about three times as long
as it is wide cannot last more than a moment;
because if one end were to
contract ever so little the
pressure there would increase,
and the narrow end would
blow air into the wider end
(Fig. 34), until the sides of
the narrow end met one
another.   The exact length
of the longest cylinder that
is stable, is a little more than
three diameters.   The cylinder
just becomes unstable when
its length is equal to its cir-
cumference, and this is $3\frac{1}{7}$
diameters almost exactly.

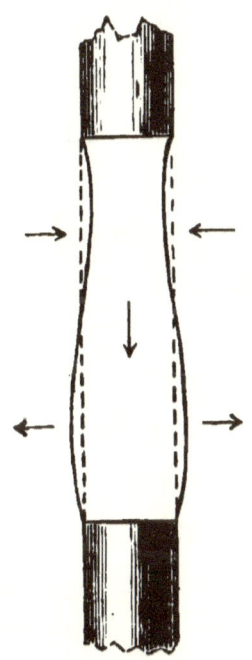

Fig. 34.

I will gradually separate these rings, keeping up a supply of air, and you will see
that when the tube gets nearly three times
as long as it is wide it is getting very difficult to manage, and then suddenly it grows
a waist nearer one end than the other, and

breaks off forming a pair of separate and unequal bubbles.

If now you have a cylinder of liquid of great length suddenly formed and left to itself, it clearly cannot retain that form. It must break up into a series of drops. Unfortunately the changes go on so quickly in a falling stream of water that no one by merely looking at it could follow the movements of the separate drops, but I hope to be able to show to you in two or three ways exactly what is happening. You may remember that we were able to make a large drop of one liquid in another, because in this way the effect of the weight was neutralized, and as large drops oscillate or change their shape much more slowly than small, it is more easy to see what is happening. I have in this glass box water coloured blue on which is floating paraffin, made heavier by mixing with it a bad-smelling and dangerous liquid called bisulphide of carbon.

The water is only a very little heavier than the mixture. If I now dip a pipe into the water and let it fill, I can then raise it and allow drops to slowly form. Drops as large as a shilling are now forming, and when each one has reached its full size, a neck forms above it, which is drawn out by the falling drop into a little cylinder. You will notice that the liquid of the neck has gathered it- self into a little drop which falls away just after the large drop. The action is now going on so slowly that you can follow it. Fig. 35 con- tains forty-three consecutive views of the growth and fall of the drop taken photographic- ally at intervals of one-twen- tieth of a second. For the use to which this figure is to be put, see page 149. If I again fill the pipe with water, and this time draw it rapidly out of the liquid, I shall leave behind a cylinder which will break up into balls, as you can easily see (Fig. 36). I should like now to show you, as I have this apparatus in its place, that you can blow bubbles of water

See Diagram at the end of the Book.

Fig. 35.

F

containing paraffin in the paraffin mixture,

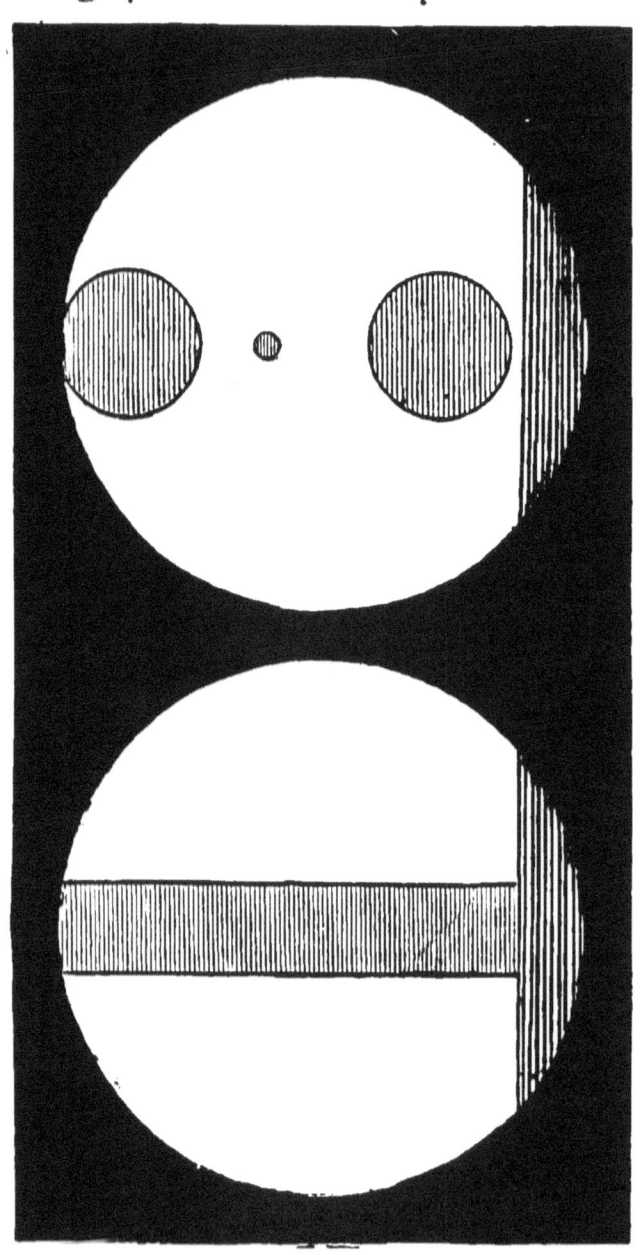

Fig. 36.

and you will see some which have other
bubbles and drops of one or other liquid inside
again. One of these compound bubble drops
is now resting stationary on a heavier layer of
liquid, so that you can see it all the better

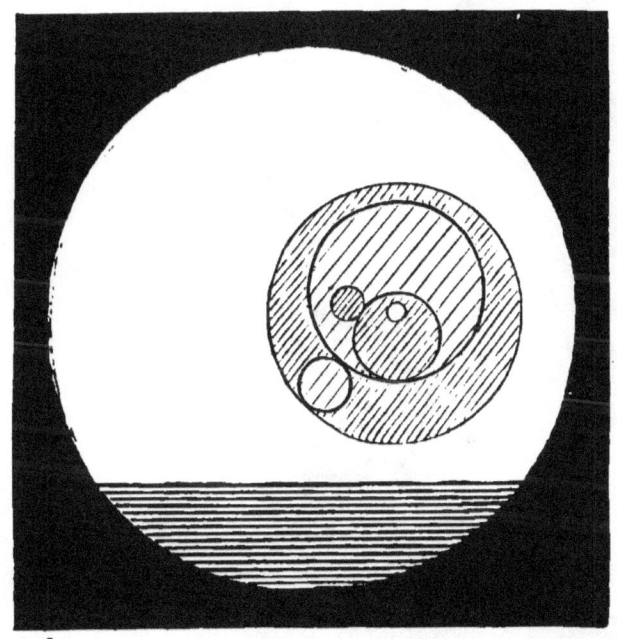

Fig. 37.

(Fig. 37). If I rapidly draw the pipe out of
the box I shall leave a long cylindrical bubble
of water containing paraffin, and this, as was
the case with the water-cylinder, slowly breaks
up into spherical bubbles.

Having now shown that a very large liquid

cylinder breaks up regularly into drops, I shall next go the other extreme, and take as an example an excessively fine cylinder. You see

Fig. 38.

a photograph of a spider on her geometrical web (Fig. 38). If I had time I should like to tell you how the spider goes to work to make this beautiful structure, and a great deal about these wonderful creatures, but I must do no more than show you that there are two kinds of web—those that point outwards, which are hard and smooth, and those that go round and round, which are very elastic, and which are covered with beads of a sticky liquid. Now there are in a good web over a quarter of a million of these beads which catch the flies for the spider's dinner. A spider makes a whole web in an hour, and generally has to make a new one every day. She would not be able to go round and stick all these in place, even if she knew how, because she would not have time. Instead of this she makes use of the way that a liquid cylinder breaks up into beads as follows. She spins a thread, and at the same time wets it with a sticky liquid, which of course is at first a cylinder. This cannot remain a cylinder, but breaks up into beads, as the photograph taken with a microscope from a real web beautifully shows (Fig. 39). You see the alternate large and small drops, and sometimes you even see extra small drops between these again. In order that you may see exactly how large these beads really are, I have placed alongside a scale of thousandths of an inch, which was photographed at the same time. To prove to you that this is what happens, I shall now show you a web that I have made myself by stroking a quartz fibre with a straw dipped in castor-oil. The same alternate large and small beads are again visible just as perfect as they were in the spider's web. In fact it is impossible to distinguish between one of my beaded webs and a spider's by looking at them. And there is this additional similarity—my webs are just as good as a spider's for catching flies. You might say that a large cylinder of water in oil, or a microscopic cylinder on a thread, is not the same as an ordinary jet of water, and that you would like to see if it be-

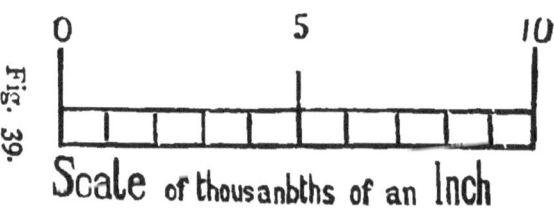

Fig. 39.

Scale of thousanbths of an Inch

haves as I have described. The next photograph (Fig. 40), taken by the light of an instantaneous electric spark, and magnified three and a quarter times, shows a fine column of water falling from a jet. You will now see that it is at first a cylinder, that as it goes down necks and bulges begin to form, and at last beads separate, and you can see the little drops as well. The beads also vibrate, becoming alternately long and wide, and there can be no doubt that the sparkling portion of a jet, though it appears continuous, is really made up of beads which pass so rapidly before the eye that it is impossible to follow them. (I should explain that for a reason which will appear later, I made a loud note by whistling into a key at the time that this photograph was taken.)

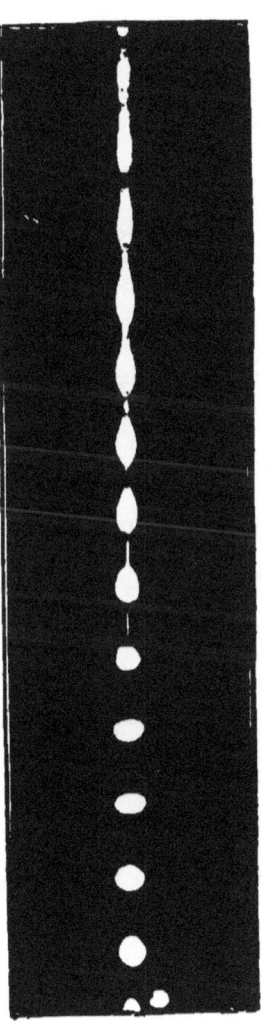

Fig. 40.

Lord Rayleigh has shown that in a stream of water one twenty-fifth of an inch in diameter, necks impressed upon the stream, even though imperceptible, develop a thousandfold in depth every fortieth of a second, and thus it is not difficult to understand that in such a stream the water is already broken through before it has fallen many inches. He has also shown that free water drops vibrate at a rate which may be found as follows. A drop two inches in diameter makes one complete vibration in one second. If the diameter is reduced to one quarter of its amount, the time of vibration will be reduced to one-eighth, or if the diameter is reduced to one-hundredth, the time will be reduced to one-thousandth, and so on. The same relation between the diameter and the time of breaking up applies also to cylinders. We can at once see how fast a bead of water the size of one of those in the spider's web would vibrate if pulled out of shape, and let go suddenly. If we take the diameter as being one eight-hundredth of an inch, and it is really even finer, then the bead would have a diameter of one sixteen-hundredth of a two-inch bead, which makes one vibration in one second. It will therefore vibrate sixty-four thousand times as fast, or sixty-four thousand times a second. Water-drops the size of the little beads, with a diameter of rather less than one three-thousandth of an inch, would vibrate half a million times a second, under the sole influence of the feebly elastic skin of water! We thus see how powerful is the influence of the feebly elastic water-skin on drops of water that are sufficiently small.

I shall now cause a small fountain to play, and shall allow the water as it falls to patter upon a sheet of paper. You can see both the fountain itself and its shadow upon the screen. You will notice that the water comes out of the nozzle as a smooth cylinder, that it presently begins to glitter, and that the separate drops scatter over a great space (Fig. 41). Now why should the drops scatter? All the water comes out of the jet at the same rate and starts in the same direction, and yet after a short way the separate drops by no means follow the same paths. Now instead of explaining this, and then showing experiments to test the truth of the explanation, I shall reverse the usual order, and show one or two experiments first, which

I think you will all agree are so like magic, so wonderful are they and yet so simple, that if they had been performed a few hundred years ago, the rash person who showed them

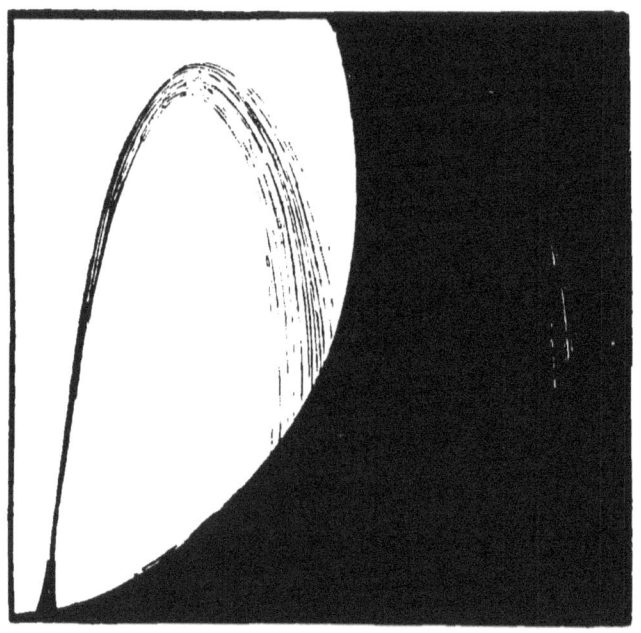

Fig. 41.

might have run a serious risk of being burnt alive.

You now see the water of the jet scattering in all directions, and you hear it making a pattering sound on the paper on which it falls. I take out of my pocket a stick of sealing-wax and instantly all is changed, even though I am some way off and can touch nothing. The water ceases to scatter; it travels in one continuous line (Fig. 42), and falls upon the paper making a loud rattling noise which must remind you of the rain of a thunder-storm.

Fig. 42.

I come a little nearer to the fountain and the water scatters again, but this time in quite a different way. The falling drops are much larger than they were before. Directly I hide the sealing-wax the jet of water recovers its old appearance, and as soon as the sealing-wax is taken out it travels in a single line again.

Now instead of the sealing-wax I shall take a smoky flame easily made by dipping some cotton-wool on the end of a stick into benzine, and lighting it. As long as the flame is held away from the fountain it produces no effect, but the instant that I bring it near so that the water passes through the flame, the fountain ceases to scatter; it all runs in one line and falls in a dirty black stream upon the paper. Ever so little oil fed into the jet from a tube as fine as a hair does exactly the same thing.

I shall now set a tuning-fork sounding at the other side of the table. The fountain has not altered in appearance. I now touch the stand of the tuning-fork with a long stick which rests against the nozzle. Again the water gathers itself together even more perfectly than before, and the paper upon which it falls is humming out a note which is the same as that produced by the tuning-fork. If I alter the rate at which the water flows you will see that the appearance is changed again, but it is never like a jet which is not acted upon by a musical sound. Sometimes the fountain breaks up

into two or three and sometimes many more
distinct lines, as though it came out of as many
tubes of different sizes and pointing in slightly
different directions (Fig. 43). The effect of
different notes could be very easily shown if
any one were to sing to the piece of wood by

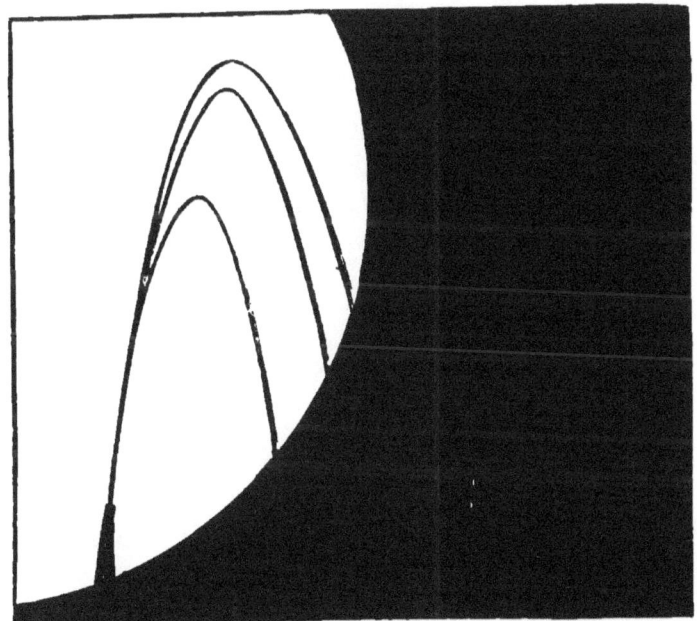

Fig. 43.

which the jet is held. I can make noises of
different pitches, which for this purpose are
perhaps better than musical notes, and you
can see that with every new noise the fountain
puts on a different appearance. You may well

wonder how these trifling influences—sealing-wax, the smoky flame, or the more or less musical noise—should produce this mysterious result, but the explanation is not so difficult as you might expect.

I hope to make this clear when we meet again.

LECTURE III.

At the conclusion of the last lecture I showed you some curious experiments with a fountain of water, which I have now to explain. Consider what I have said about a liquid cylinder. If it is a little more than three times as long as it is wide, it cannot retain its form; if it is made very much more than three times as long, it will break up into a series of beads. Now, if in any way a series of necks could be developed upon a cylinder which were less than three diameters apart, some of them would tend to heal up, because a piece of a cylinder less than three diameters long is stable. If they were about three diameters apart, the form being then unstable, the necks would get more pronounced in time, and would at last break through, so that beads would be formed. If necks were made at distances more than three diameters apart, then the cylinder would go on breaking up by the narrowing of these

necks, and it would most easily break up into
drops when the necks were just four and a half
diameters apart.   In other words, if a fountain
were to issue from a nozzle held perfectly still,
the water would most easily break into beads at
the distance of four and a half diameters apart,
but it would break up into a greater number
closer together, or a smaller number further
apart, if by slight disturbances of the jet very
slight waists were impressed upon the issuing
cylinder of water.   When you make a fountain
play from a jet which you hold as still as
possible, there are still accidental tremors of all
kinds, which impress upon the issuing cylinder
slightly narrow and wide places at irregular distances, and so the cylinder breaks up irregu-
larly into drops of different sizes and at different distances apart.   Now these drops, as they
are in the act of separating from one another,
and are drawing out the waist, as you have
seen, are being pulled for the moment towards
one another by the elasticity of the skin of the
waist; and, as they are free in the air to move
as they will, this will cause the hinder one to
hurry on, and the more forward one to lag
behind, so that unless they are all exactly

alike both in size and distance apart they will
many of them bounce together before long.
You would expect when they hit one another
afterwards that they would join, but I shall be
able to show you in a moment that they do
not; they act like two india-rubber balls, and
bounce away again.   Now it is not difficult to
see that if you have a series of drops of different sizes and at irregular distances bouncing
against one another frequently, they will tend
to separate and to fall, as we have seen, on all
parts of the paper down below.   What did
the sealing-wax or the smoky flame do? and
what can the musical sound do to stop this
from happening?   Let me first take the
sealing-wax.   A piece of sealing-wax rubbed
on your coat is electrified, and will attract light
bits of paper up to it.   The sealing-wax acts
electrically on the different water-drops, causing
them to attract one another, feebly, it is true,
but with sufficient power where they meet to
make them break through the air-film between
them and join.   To show that this is no fancy,
I have now in front of the lantern two fountains of clean water coming from separate
bottles, and you can see that they bounce

G

apart perfectly (Fig. 44). To show that they do really bounce, I have coloured the water in the two bottles differently. The sealing-wax is now in my pocket; I shall retire to the other side of the room, and the instant it appears

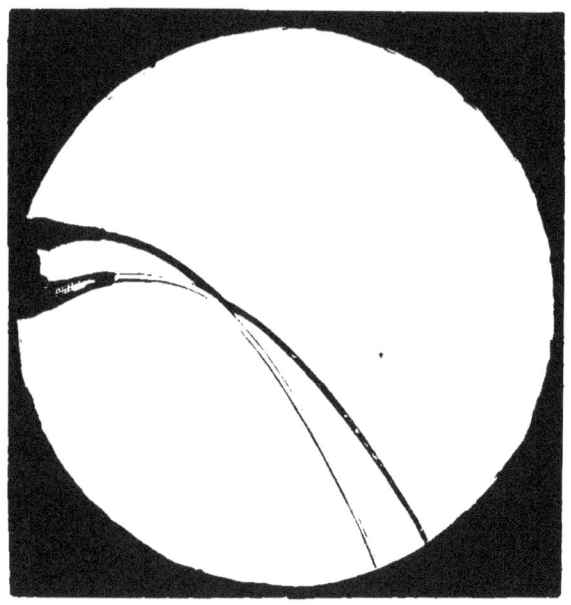

Fig. 44.

the jets of water coalesce (Fig. 45). This may be repeated as often as you like, and it never fails. These two bouncing jets are in fact one of the most delicate tests for the presence of electricity that exist. You are now able to understand the first experiment. The

separate drops which bounced away from one
another, and scattered in all directions, are
unable to bounce when the sealing-wax is held
up, because of its electrical action. They
therefore unite, and the result is, that instead

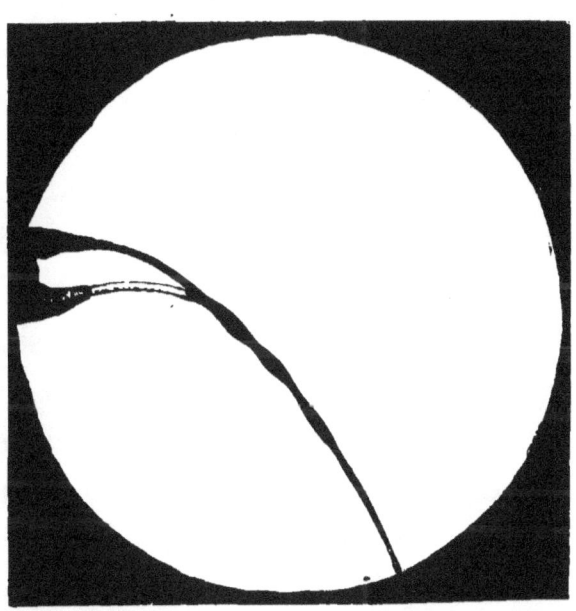

Fig. 45.

of a great number of little drops falling all
over the paper, the stream pours in a single
line, and great drops, such as you see in a
thunder-storm, fall on the top of one another.
There can be no doubt that it is for this reason
that the drops of rain in a thunder-storm are

so large. This experiment and its explanation are due to Lord Rayleigh.

The smoky flame, as lately shown by Mr. Bidwell, does the same thing. The reason probably is that the dirt breaks through the air-film, just as dust in the air will make the two fountains join as they did when they were electrified. However, it is possible that oily matter condensed on the water may have something to do with the effect observed, because oil alone acts quite as well as a flame, but the action of oil in this case, as when it smooths a stormy sea, is not by any means so easily understood.

When I held the sealing-wax closer, the drops coalesced in the same way; but they were then so much more electrified that they repelled one another as similarly electrified bodies are known to do, and so the electrical scattering was produced.

You possibly already see why the tuning-fork made the drops follow in one line, but I shall explain. A musical note is, as is well known, caused by a rapid vibration; the more rapid the vibration the higher is the pitch of the note. For instance, I have a tooth-wheel which I can turn round very rapidly if I wish. Now that it is turning slowly you can hear the separate teeth knocking against a card that I am holding in the other hand. I am now turning faster, and the card is giving out a note of a low pitch. As I make the wheel turn faster and faster, the pitch of the note gradually rises, and it would, if I could only turn fast enough, give so high a note that we should not be able to hear it. A tuning-fork vibrates at a certain definite rate, and therefore gives a definite note. The fork now sounding vibrates 128 times in every second. The nozzle, therefore, is made to vibrate, but almost imperceptibly, 128 times a second, and to impress upon the issuing cylinder of water 128 imperceptible waists every second. Now it just depends what size the jet is, and how fast the water is issuing, whether these waists are about four and a half diameters apart in the cylinder. If the jet is larger, the water must pass more quickly, or under a greater pressure, for this to be the case; if the jet is finer, a smaller speed will be sufficient. If it should happen that the waists so made are anywhere. about four diameters apart, then

even though they are so slightly developed
that if you had an exact drawing of them, you
would not be able to detect the slightest change
of diameter, they will grow at a great speed,
and therefore the water column will break up
regularly, every drop will be like the one
behind it, and like the one in front of it, and
not all different, as is the case when the breaking of the water merely depends upon accidental tremors. If the drops then are all alike
in every respect, of course they all follow the
same path, and so appear to fall in a continuous
stream.   If the waists are about four and a
half diameters apart, then the jet will break up
most easily; but it will, as I have said, break
up under the influence of a considerable range
of notes, which cause the waists to be formed
at other distances, provided they are more
than three diameters apart. If two notes are
sounded at the same time, then very often
each will produce its own effect, and the result
is the alternate formation of drops of different
sizes, which then make the jet divide into two
separate streams.   In this way, three, four, or
even many more distinct streams may be
produced.

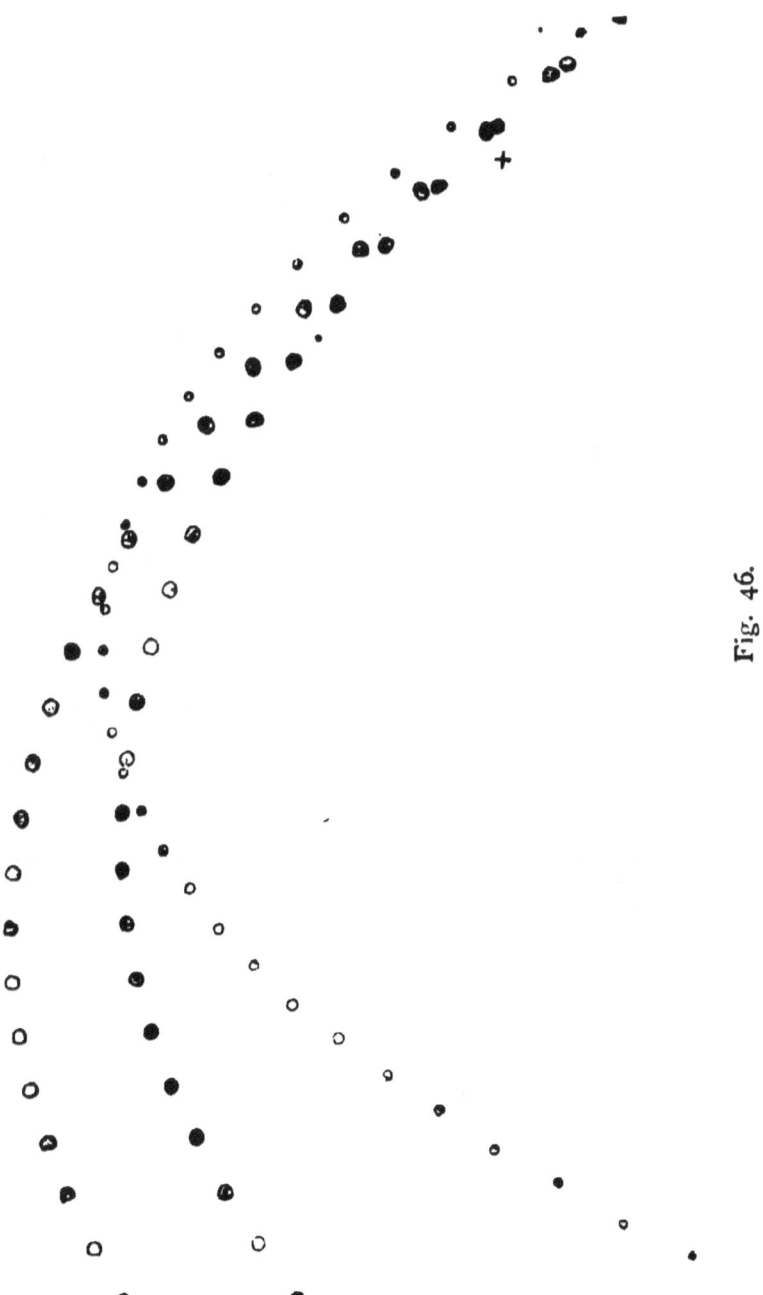

Fig. 46.

I can now show you photographs of some
of these musical fountains, taken by the instantaneous flash of an electric spark, and you can
see the separate paths described by the drops
of different sizes (Fig. 46). In one photograph
there are eight distinct fountains all breaking
from the same jet, but following quite distinct
paths, each of which is clearly marked out by a
perfectly regular series of drops. You can also
in these photographs see drops actually in the
act of bouncing against one another, and flattened when they meet, as if they were india-
rubber balls. In the photograph now upon
the screen the effect of this rebound, which
occurs at the place marked with a cross, is to
hurry on the upper and more forward drop,
and to retard the other one, and so to make
them travel with slightly different velocities
and directions. It is for this reason that they
afterwards follow distinct paths. The smaller
drops had no doubt been acted on in a similar
way, but the part of the fountain where this
happened was just outside the photographic
plate, and so there is no record of what
occurred. The very little drops of which I
have so often spoken are generally thrown out

from the side of a fountain of water under the influence of a musical sound, after which they describe regular little curves of their own, quite distinct from the main stream. They, of course, can only get out sideways after one or two bouncings from the regular drops in front and behind. You can easily show that they are really formed below the place where they first appear, by taking a piece of electrified sealing-wax and holding it near the stream close to the nozzle and gradually raising it. When it comes opposite to the place where the little drops are really formed, it will act on them more powerfully than on the large drops, and immediately pull them out from a place where the moment before none seemed to exist. They will then circulate in perfect little orbits round the sealing-wax, just as the planets do round the sun; but in this case, being met by the resistance of the air, the orbits are spirals, and the little drops after many revolutions ultimately fall upon the wax, just as the planets would fall into the sun after many revolutions, if their motion through space were interfered with by friction of any kind.

There is only one thing needed to make the

demonstration of the behaviour of a musical jet complete, and that is, that you should yourselves see these drops in their different positions in an actual fountain of water. Now if I were to produce a powerful electric spark, then it is true that some of you might for an instant catch sight of the drops, but I do not think that most would see anything at all. But if, instead of making merely one flash, I were to make another when each drop had just travelled to the position which the one in front of it occupied before, and then another when each drop had moved on one place again, and so on, then all the drops, at the moments that the flashes of light fell upon them, would occupy the same positions, and thus all these drops would appear fixed in the air, though of course they really are travelling fast enough. If, however, I do not quite succeed in keeping exact time with my flashes of light, then a curious appearance will be produced. Suppose, for instance, that the flashes of light follow one another rather too quickly, then each drop will not have had quite time enough to get to its proper place at each flash, and thus at the second flash all the drops will be seen in positions which are just behind those which they occupied at the first flash, and in the same way at the third flash they will be seen still further behind their former places, and so on, and therefore they will appear to be moving slowly backwards; whereas if my flashes do not follow quite quickly enough, then the drops will, every time that there is a flash, have travelled just a little too far, and so they will all appear to be moving slowly forwards. Now let us try the experiment. There is the electric lantern sending a powerful beam of light on to the screen. This I bring to a focus with a lens, and then let it pass through a small hole in a piece of card. The light then spreads out and falls upon the screen. The fountain of water is between the card and the screen, and so a shadow is cast which is conspicuous enough. Now I place just behind the card a little electric motor, which will make a disc of card which has six holes near the edge spin round very fast. The holes come one after the other opposite the hole in the fixed card, and so at every turn six flashes of light are produced. When the card is turning about $21\frac{1}{2}$ times a second, then the flashes will follow one another at the

right rate. I have now started the motor,
and after a moment or two I shall have
obtained the right speed, and this I know by
blowing through the holes, when a musical
note will be produced, higher than the fork if
the speed is too high, and lower than the
fork if the speed is too low, and exactly the
same as the fork if it is right.

To make it still more evident when the
speed is exactly right, I have placed the tuning-
fork also between the light and the screen, so
that you may see it illuminated, and its shadow
upon the screen. I have not yet allowed the
water to flow, but I want you to look at the
fork. For a moment I have stopped the
motor, so that the light may be steady, and
you can see that the fork is in motion because
its legs appear blurred at the ends, where of
course the motion is most rapid. Now the
motor is started, and almost at once the fork
appears quite different. It now looks like
a piece of india-rubber, slowly opening and
shutting, and now it appears quite still, but the
noise it is making shows that it is not still by
any means. The legs of the fork are vibrating,
but the light only falls upon them at regular

intervals, which correspond with their movement, and so, as I explained in the case of the
water-drops, the fork appears perfectly still.
Now the speed is slightly altered, and, as I
have explained, each new flash of light, coming
just too soon or just too late, shows the fork
in a position which is just before or just behind
that made visible by the previous flash. You
thus see the fork slowly going through its
evolutions, though of course in reality the legs
are moving backwards and forwards 128 times
a second. By looking at the fork or its
shadow, you will therefore be able to tell
whether the light is keeping exact time with
the vibrations, and therefore with the water-
drops.

Now the water is running, and you see all
the separate drops apparently stationary, strung
like pearls or beads of silver upon an invisible
wire (see Frontispiece). If I make the card
turn ever so little more slowly, then all the
drops will appear to slowly march onwards, and
what is so beautiful,—but I am afraid few will
see this,—each little drop may be seen to gradually break off, pulling out a waist which becomes
a little drop, and then when the main drop is

free it slowly oscillates, becoming wide and long, or turning over and over, as it goes on its way. If it so happens that a double or multiple jet is being produced, then you can see the little drops moving up to one another, squeezing each other where they meet and bouncing away again. Now the card is turning a little too fast and the drops appear to be moving backwards, so that it seems as if the water is coming up out of the tank on the floor, quietly going over my head, down into the nozzle, and so back to the water-supply of the place. Of course this is not happening at all, as you know very well, and as you will see if I simply try and place my finger between two of these drops. The splashing of the water in all directions shows that it is not moving quite so quietly as it appears. There is one more thing that I would mention about this experiment. Every time that the flashing light gains or loses one complete flash, upon the motion of the tuning-fork, it will appear to make one complete oscillation, and the water-drops will appear to move back or on one place.

I must now come to one of the most beautiful applications of these musical jets

to practical purposes which it is possible to
imagine, and what I shall now show are a few
out of a great number of the experiments of
Mr. Chichester Bell, cousin of Mr. Graham
Bell, the inventor of the telephone.

To begin with I have a very small jet of
water forced through the nozzle at a great
pressure, as you can see if I point it towards
the ceiling, as the water rises eight or ten feet.
If I allow this stream of water to fall upon
an india-rubber sheet, stretched over the end
of a tube as big as my little finger, then the
little sheet will be depressed by the water, and
the more so if the stream is strong. Now
if I hold the jet close to the sheet the smooth
column of liquid will press the sheet steadily,
and it will remain quiet; but if I gradually
take the jet further away from the sheet, then
any waists that may have been formed in the
liquid column, which grow as they travel, will
make their existence perfectly evident. When
a wide part of the column strikes the sheet it
will be depressed rather more than usual, and
when a narrow part follows, the depression will
be less. In other words, any very slight
vibration imparted to the jet will be magnified

by the growth of waists, and the sheet of india-
rubber will reproduce the vibration, but on a
magnified scale. Now if you remember that
sound consists of vibrations, then you will
understand that a jet is a machine for magnify-
ing sound. To show that this is the case I am
now directing the jet on to the sheet, and you
can hear nothing; but I shall hold a piece of
wood against the nozzle, and now, if on the
whole the jet tends to break up at any one rate
rather than at any other, or if the wood or the
sheet of rubber will vibrate at any rate most
easily, then the first few vibrations which correspond to this rate will be imparted to the
wood, which will impress them upon the nozzle
and so upon the cylinder of liquid, where they
will become magnified; the result is that the
jet immediately begins to sing of its own
accord, giving out a loud note (Fig. 47).

I will now remove the piece of wood. On
placing against the nozzle an ordinary lever
watch, the jolt which is imparted to the case
at every tick, though it is so small that you
cannot detect it, jolts the nozzle also, and thus
causes a neck to form in the jet of water which
will grow as it travels, and so produce a loud

tick, audible in every part of this large room (Fig. 48).   Now I want you to notice how the vibration is magnified by the action I have described.   I now hold the nozzle close to the rubber sheet, and you can hear nothing.   As I

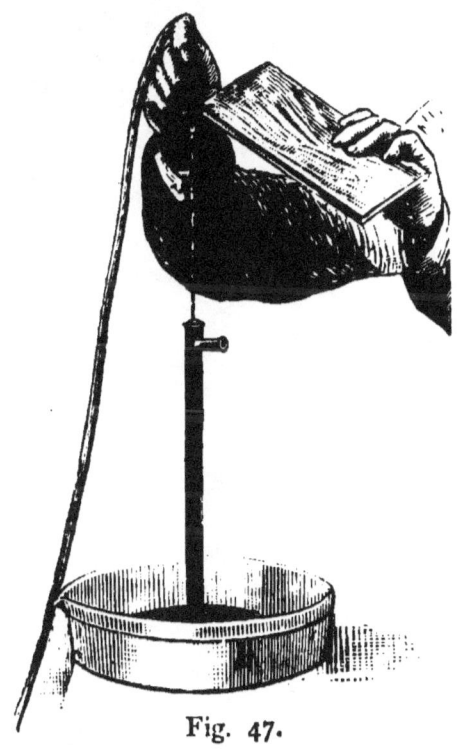

Fig. 47.

gradually raise it a faint echo is produced, which gradually gets louder and louder, until at last it is more like a hammer striking an anvil than the tick of a watch.

I shall now change this watch for another

H

which, thanks to a friend, I am able to use.
This watch is a repeater, that is, if you press
upon a nob it will strike, first the hour, then
the quarters, and then the minutes. I think the

Fig. 48.

water-jet will enable you all to hear what time
it is. Listen! one, two, three, four; . . . ting-
tang, ting-tang; . . . one, two, three, four, five,
six. Six minutes after half-past four. You
notice that not only did you hear the number
of strokes, but the jet faithfully reproduced the

musical notes, so that you could distinguish one note from the others.

I can in the same way make the jet play a tune by simply making the nozzle rest against a long stick, which is pressed upon a musical-box. The musical-box is carefully shut up in a double box of thick felt, and you can hardly hear anything; but the moment that the nozzle is made to rest against the stick and the water is directed upon the india-rubber sheet, the sound of the box is loudly heard, I hope, in every part of the room. It is usual to describe a fountain as playing, but it is now evident that a fountain can even play a tune. There is, however, one peculiarity which is perfectly evident. The jet breaks up at certain rates more easily than at others, or, in other words, it will respond to certain sounds in preference to others. You can hear that as the musical-box plays, certain notes are emphasized in a curious way, producing much the same effect that follows if you lay a penny upon the upper strings of a horizontal piano.

Now, on returning to our soap-bubbles, you may remember that I stated that the cate-noid and the plane were the only figures of revolution which had no curvature, and which therefore produced no pressure. There are plenty of other surfaces which are apparently curved in all directions and yet have no curvature, and which therefore produce no pressure; but these are not figures of revolution, that is,

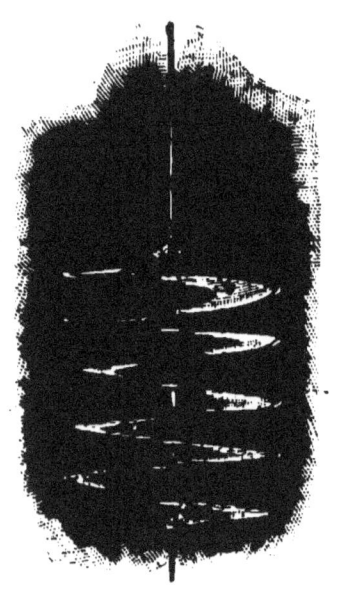

they cannot be obtained by simply spinning a curved line about an axis. These may be produced in any quantity by making wire frames of various shapes and dipping them in soap and water. On taking them out a wonderful variety of surfaces of no curvature will be seen. One such surface is that known as the screw-surface. To produce this it

Fig. 49.

is only necessary to take a piece of wire wound a few times in an open helix (commonly called spiral), and to bend the two ends so as to meet a second wire passing down the centre. The screw-surface developed by dipping this frame in soap-water is well worth seeing (Fig. 49). It is impossible to give any idea of the perfection of the form in a figure, but fortunately this is an experiment which any one can easily perform.

Then again, if a wire frame is made in the shape of the edges of any of the regular geometrical solids, very beautiful figures will

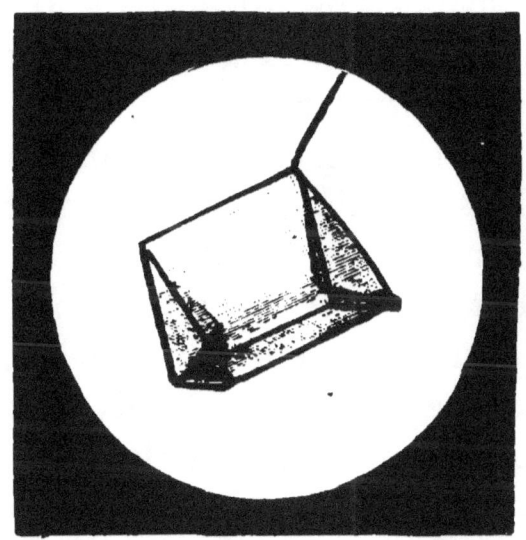

Fig. 50.

be found upon them after they have been dipped in soap-water. In the case of the triangular prism these surfaces are all flat, and at the edges where these planes meet one another there are always three meeting each other at equal angles (Fig. 50). This, owing to the fact that the frame is three-sided, is not surprising. After looking at this three-sided frame with three films meeting down the central line, you might expect that with a four-sided or square frame there would be four films meeting each other in a line down the middle. But it is a curious thing that it does not matter how irregular the frame may be, or how complicated a mass of froth may be, there can never be more than three films meeting in an edge, or more than four edges, or six films, meeting in a point. Moreover the films and edges can only meet one another at equal angles. If for a moment by any accident four films do meet in the same edge, or if the angles are not exactly equal, then the form, whatever it may be, is unstable; it cannot last, but the films slide over one another and never rest until they have settled down into a position in which the conditions of stability are fulfilled. This may be illustrated by a very simple experiment which you can easily try at home, and which you can now see projected upon the screen. There are two pieces of window-glass about half an inch apart, which form the sides of a sort of box into which some soap and water have been poured.

On blowing through a pipe which is immersed
in the water, a great number of bubbles are
formed between the plates. If the bubbles are
all large enough to reach across from one plate
to the other, you will at once see that there
are nowhere more than three films meeting
one another, and where they meet the angles
are all equal. The curvature of the bubbles
makes it difficult to see at first that the angles
really are all alike, but if you only look at a
very short piece close to where they meet, and
so avoid being bewildered by the curvature,
you will see that what I have said is true.
You will also see, if you are quick, that when
the bubbles are blown, sometimes four for a
moment do meet, but that then the films at
once slide over one another and settle down into
their only possible position of rest (Fig. 51).

The air inside a bubble is generally under
pressure, which is produced by its elasticity
and curvature. If the bubble would let the
air pass through it from one side to the other
of course it would soon shut up, as it did when
a ring was hung upon one, and the film within
the ring was broken. But there are no holes
in a bubble, and so you would expect that a

gas like air could not pass through to the
other side. Nevertheless it is a fact that gases
can slowly get through to the other side, and in
the case of certain vapours the process is far
more rapid than any one would think possible.

Ether produces a vapour which is very heavy,

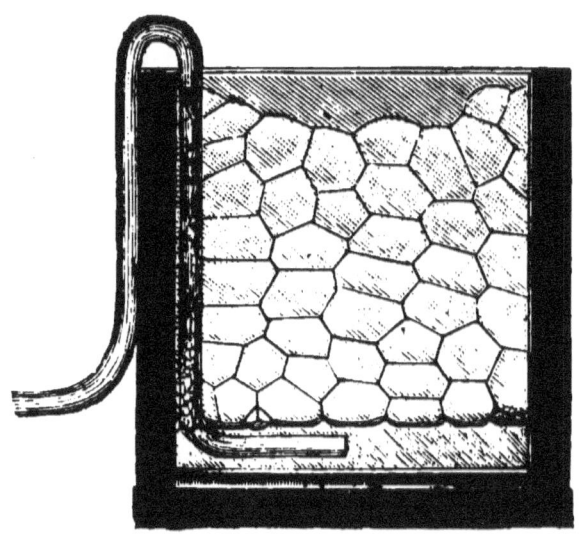

Fig. 51.

and which also burns very easily. This vapour
can get to the other side of a bubble almost
at once. I shall pour a little ether upon blotting-paper in this bell jar, and fill the jar with
its heavy vapour. You can see that the jar
is filled with something, not by looking at it,
for it appears empty, but by looking at its

shadow on the screen. Now I tilt it gently
to one side, and you see something pouring
out of it, which is the vapour of ether. It is
easy to show that this is heavy; it is only
necessary to drop into the jar a bubble, and
so soon as the bubble meets the heavy vapour
it stops falling and remains floating upon the
surface as a cork does
upon water (Fig. 52).
Now let me test the
bubble and see whether
any of the vapour has
passed to the inside. I
pick it up out of the jar
with a wire ring and carry
it to a light, and at once
there is a burst of flame.
But this is not sufficient
to show that the ether
vapour has passed to the inside, because it
might have condensed in sufficient quantity
upon the bubble to make it inflammable.
You remember that when I poured some of
this vapour upon water in the first lecture,
sufficient condensed to so weaken the water-
skin that the frame of wire could get through

Fig. 52.

to the other side. However, I can see whether this is the true explanation or not by blowing a bubble on a wide pipe, and holding it in the vapour for a moment. Now on removing it you notice that the bubble hangs

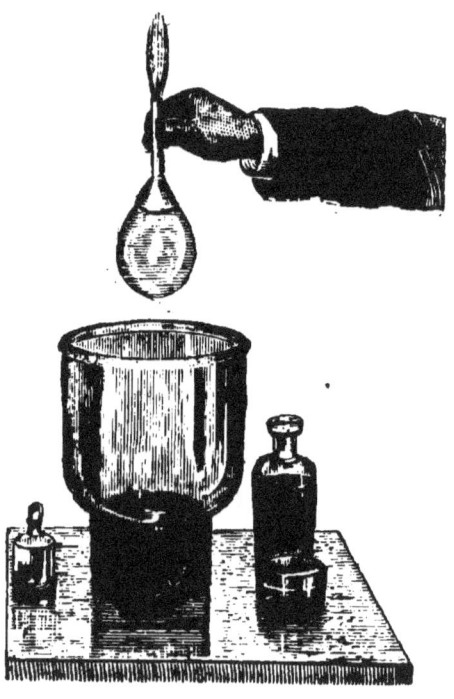

Fig. 53.

like a heavy drop; it has lost the perfect roundness that it had at first, and this looks as if the vapour had found its way in, but this is made certain by bringing a light to the mouth of the tube, when the vapour, forced

out by the elasticity of the bubble, catches
fire and burns with a flame five or six inches
long (Fig. 53). You might also have noticed
that when the bubble was removed, the vapour
inside it began to pass out again and fell
away in a heavy stream, but this you could
only see by looking at the shadow upon the
screen.

You may have noticed when I made the
drops of oil in the mixture of alcohol and
water, that when they were brought together
they did not at once unite; they pressed against
one another and pushed each other away if
allowed, just as the water-drops did in the
fountain of which I showed you a photograph.
You also may have noticed that the drops of
water in the paraffin mixture bounced against
one another, or if filled with the paraffin, formed
bubbles in which often other small drops, both
of water and paraffin, remained floating.

In all these cases there was a thin film of
something between the drops which they were
unable to squeeze out, namely, water, paraffin,
or air, as the case might be. Will two soap-
bubbles also when knocked together be unable
to squeeze out the air between them? This

you can try at home just as well as I can here, but I will perform the experiment at once. I have blown a pair of bubbles, and now when I hit them together they remain distinct and separate (Fig. 54).

I shall next place a bubble on a ring, which it is just too large to get through. In my hand I hold a ring, on which I have a flat

Fig. 54.

film, made by placing a bubble upon it and breaking it on one side. If I gently press the bubble with the flat film, I can push it through the ring to the other side (Fig. 55), and yet the two have not really touched one another at all. The bubble can be pushed backwards and forwards in this way many times.

I have now blown a bubble and hung it below a ring. To this bubble I can hang another ring of thin wire, which pulls it a little out of shape. Since the pressure inside is less than that corresponding to a complete sphere, and since it is greater than that outside, and this we can tell by looking at the caps, the curve is

Fig. 55.

part of one of those represented by the dotted lines in C or E, Fig. 31. However, without considering the curve any more, I shall push the end of the pipe inside, and blow another bubble there, and let it go. It falls gently

until it rests upon the outer bubble; not at
the bottom, because the heavy ring keeps that

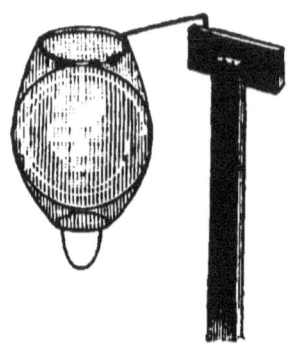

Fig. 56.

part out of reach, but along
a circular line higher up
(Fig. 56). I can now drain
away the heavy drops of
liquid from below the
bubbles with a pipe, and
leave them clean and
smooth all over. I can
now pull the lower ring

down, squeezing the inner bubble into a shape
like an egg (Fig. 57), or swing it round and

Fig. 57.

round, and then with a little
care peel away the ring
from off the bubble, and
leave them both perfectly
round every way (Fig. 58).
I can draw out the air from
the outer bubble till you
can hardly see between
them, and then blow in,
and the harder I blow, the
more is it evident that the

two bubbles are not touching at all; the
inner one is now spinning round and round

in the very centre of the large bubble, and finally, on breaking the outer one the inner floats away, none the worse for its very unusual treatment.

There is a pretty variation of the last experiment, which, however, requires that a little green dye called fluorescine, or better, uranine, should be dissolved in a separate dish of the soap-water. Then you can blow the outer bubble with clean soap-water, and the inner one with the coloured water. Then if you look at the two bubbles by ordin-

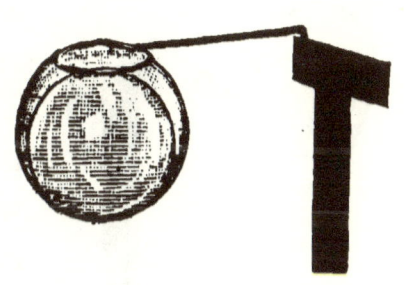

Fig. 58.

ary light, you will hardly notice any difference; but if you allow sunlight, or electric light from an arc lamp, to shine upon them, the inner one will appear a brilliant green, while the outer one will remain clear as before. They will not mix at all, showing that though the inner one is apparently resting against the outer one, there is in reality a thin cushion of air between.

Now you know that coal-gas is lighter than air, and so a soap-bubble blown with gas,

when let go, floats up to the ceiling at once.
I shall blow a bubble on a ring with coal-gas.
It is soon evident that it is pulling upwards.
I shall go on feeding it with gas, and I want
you to notice the very beautiful shapes that
it takes (Fig. 59, but imagine the globe inside
removed). These are all exactly the curves
that a water-drop assumes when hanging from

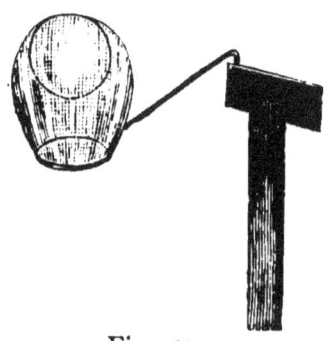

a pipe, except that they
are the other way up.
The strength of the skin
is now barely able to
withstand the pull, and
now the bubble breaks
away just as the drop of
water did.

Fig. 59.

I shall next place a bubble blown with air
upon a ring, and blow inside it a bubble
blown with a mixture of air and gas. It of
course floats up and rests against the top of
the outer bubble (Fig. 60). Now I shall let
a little gas into the outer one, until the surrounding gas is about as heavy as the inner
bubble. It now no longer rests against the
top, but floats about in the centre of the large
bubble (Fig. 61), just as the drop of oil did

in the mixture of alcohol and water. You can see that the inner bubble is really lighter than air, because if I break the outer one, the inner one rises rapidly to the ceiling.

Fig. 60.

Instead of blowing the first bubble on a heavy fixed ring, I shall now blow one on a light ring, made of very thin wire. This bubble contains only air. If I blow inside this a bubble with coal-gas, then the gas-bubble will try

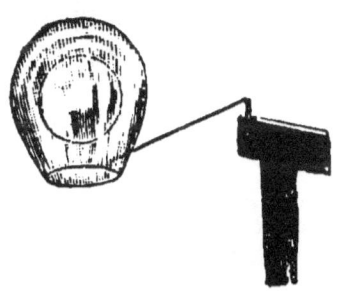

and rise, and will press against the top of the outer one with such force as to make it carry up the wire ring and a yard of cotton, and some paper to which the cotton is tied (Fig. 62); and all

Fig. 61.

this time, though it is the inner one only which tends to rise, the two bubbles are not really touching one another at all.

I have now blown an air-bubble on the fixed ring, and pushed up inside it a wire

with a ring on the end. I shall now blow
another air-bubble on this inner ring. The

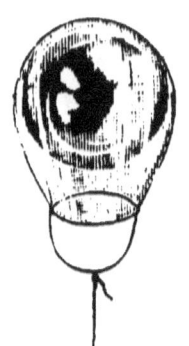

next bubble that I shall blow is
one containing gas, and this is inside the other two, and when let
go it rests against the top of the
second bubble. I next make the
second bubble a little lighter by
blowing a little gas into it, and
then make the outer one larger
with air. I can now peel off the
inner ring and take it away, leaving the two inner bubbles free,
inside the outer one (Fig. 63).
And now the multiple reflections
of the brilliant colours of the different bubbles from one to the
other, set off by the beautiful
forms which the bubbles themselves assume, give to the whole a
degree of symmetry and splendour

Fig. 62.

which you may go far to see equalled in any
other way. I have only to blow a fourth
bubble in *real* contact with the outer bubble
and the ring, to enable it to peel off and float
away with the other two inside.

We have seen that bubbles and drops be-have in very much the same way.   Let us see if electricity will produce the same effect that it did on drops.   You re-member that a piece of electrified sealing-wax prevented a fountain of water from scattering, be-cause where two drops met, instead

Fig. 63.

of bouncing, they joined together.   Now there are on these two rings bubbles which are just resting against one another, but not really touching (Fig. 64).   The instant that I take out the sealing-wax you see they join together and become one (Fig. 65).   Two soap-bubbles, therefore, enable us to detect electricity,

Fig. 64.

even when present in minute quantity, just as two water fountains did.

We can use a pair of bubbles to prove the

truth of one of the well-known actions of electricity. Inside an electrical conductor it is impossible to feel any influence of electricity outside, however much there may be, or however near you go to the surface. Let us, therefore, take the two bubbles shown in Fig. 56, and bring an electrified stick of sealing-

Fig. 65.

wax near. The outer bubble is a conductor; there is, therefore, no electrical action inside, and this you can see because, though the sealing-wax is so near the bubble that it pulls it all to one side, and though the inner one is so close to the outer one that you cannot see between them, yet the two bubbles remain separate. Had there been the slightest electrical influence inside, even to a depth of a hundred-thousandth of an inch, the two bubbles would have instantly come together.

There is one more experiment which I must show, and this will be the last; it is

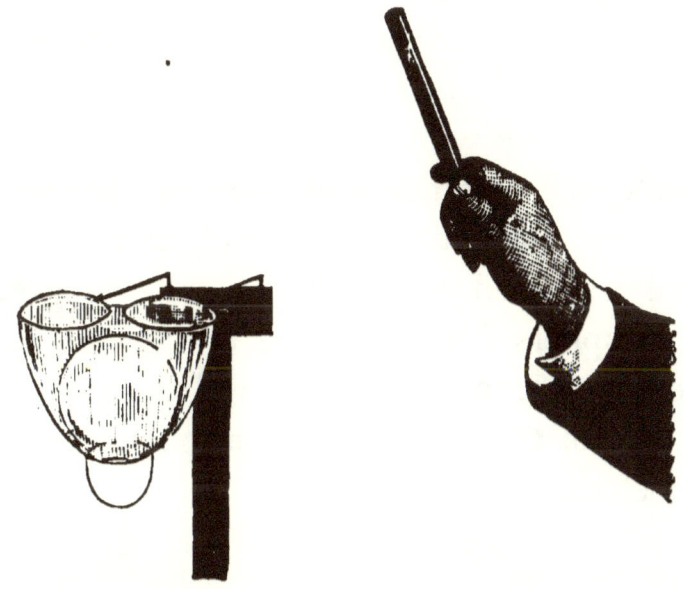

Fig. 66.

a combination of the last two, and it beautifully shows the difference between an inside and an outside bubble. I have now a plain bubble resting against the side of the pair that I have just been using. The instant that I take out the sealing-wax the two outer bubbles join, while the inner one unharmed and the heavy ring slide down to the bottom of the now single outer bubble (Fig. 66).

And now that our time has drawn to a close I must ask you whether that admiration and wonder which we all feel when we play with soap-bubbles has been destroyed by these lectures; or whether now that you know more about them it is not increased. I hope you will all agree with me that the actions upon which such common and every-day phenomena as drops and bubbles depend, actions which have occupied the attention of the greatest philosophers from the time of Newton to the present day, are not so trivial as to be unworthy of the attention of ordinary people like ourselves.

PRACTICAL HINTS.

I HOPE that the following practical hints may be found useful by those who wish themselves to successfully perform the experiments already described.

Drop with India-rubber Surface.

A sheet of thin india-rubber, about the thickness of that used in air-balls, as it appears *before* they have been blown out, must be stretched over a ring of wood or metal eighteen inches in diameter, and securely wired round the edge. The wire will hold the india-rubber better if the edge is grooved. This does not succeed if tried on a smaller scale. This experiment was shown by Sir W. Thomson at the Royal Institution.

Jumping Frame.

This is easily made by taking a light glass globe about two inches in diameter, such, for instance, as a silvered ball used to ornament a Christmas-tree or the bulb of a pipette, which is what I used. Pass through the open necks of the bulb a piece of wire about one-twentieth of an inch in diameter, and fix it permanently and water-tight upon the wire by working into the necks melted sealing-wax. An inch or two above the globe, fasten a flat frame of thin wire by soldering, or if this is too difficult, by tying and sealing-wax. A lump of lead must then be fastened or hung on to the lower end, and gradually scraped away until the wire frame will just be unable to force its way through the surface of the water. None of the dimensions or materials mentioned are of importance.

Paraffined Sieve.

Obtain a piece of copper wire gauze with about twenty wires to the inch, and cut out from it a round piece about eight inches in diameter. Lay it on a round block, of such a size that it projects about one inch all round. Then gently go round and round with the hands pressing the edge down and keeping it flat above, until the sides are evenly turned down all round. This is quite easy, because the wires can allow of the kind of distortion necessary. Then wind round the turned-up edge a few turns of thick wire to make the sides stiff. This ought to be soldered in position, but probably careful wiring will be good enough.

Melt some paraffin wax or one or two paraffin candles of the best quality in a clean flat dish, not over the fire, which would be dangerous, but on a hot plate. When melted and clear like water, dip the sieve in, and when all is hot quickly take it out and knock it once or twice on the table to shake the paraffin out of the holes. Leave upside down until cold, and then be careful not to scratch or rub off the paraffin. This had best be done in a place where a mess is of no consequence.

There is no difficulty in filling it or in setting it to float upon water.

Narrow Tubes and Capillarity.

Get some quill-glass tube from a chemist, that is, tube about the size of a pen. If it is more than, say, a foot long, cut off a piece by

first making a firm scratch in one place with
a three-cornered file, when it will break at the
place easily. To make very narrow tube from
this, hold it near the ends in the two hands
very lightly, so that the middle part is high up
in the brightest part of an ordinary bright and
flat gas flame. Keep it turning until at last
it becomes so soft that it is difficult to hold it
straight. It can then be bent into any shape,
but if it is wanted to be drawn out it must be
held still longer until the black smoke upon
it begins to crack and peel up. Then quickly
take it out of the flame, and pull the two ends
apart, when a long narrow tube will be formed
between. This can be made finer or coarser by
regulating the heat and the manner in which it
is pulled out. No directions will tell any one
so much as a very little practice. For drawing
out tubes the flame of a Bunsen burner or of
a blow-pipe is more convenient; but for bend-
ing tubes nothing is so good as the flat gas
flame. Do not clean off smoke till the tubes
are cold, and do not hurry their cooling by
wetting or blowing upon them. In the country
where gas is not to be had, the flame of a
large spirit-lamp can be made to do, but it

is not so good as a gas-flame. The narrower these tubes are, the higher will clean water be observed to rise in them. To colour the water, paints from a colour-box must not be used. They are not liquid, and will clog the very fine tubes. Some dye that will quite dissolve (as sugar does) must be used. An aniline dye, called soluble blue, does very well. A little vinegar added may make the colour last better.

Capillarity between Plates.

Two plates of flat glass, say three to five inches square, are required. Provided they are quite clean and well wetted there is no difficulty. A little soap and hot water will probably be sufficient to clean them.

Tears of Wine.

These are best seen at dessert in a glass about half filled with port. A mixture of from two to three parts of water, and one part of spirits of wine containing a very little rosaniline (a red aniline dye), to give it a nice colour, may be used, if port is not available. A piece ·

of the dye about as large as a mustard-seed
will be enough for a large wine-glass. The
sides of the glass should be wetted with the
wine.

Cat-Boxes.

Every school-boy knows how to make these.
They are not the boxes made by cutting slits
in paper. They are simply made by folding,
and are then blown out like the "frog," which
is also made of folded paper.

Liquid Beads.

Instead of melting gold, water rolled on to
a table thickly dusted with lycopodium, or
other fine dust, or quicksilver rolled or thrown
upon a smooth table, will show the difference
in the shape of large and small beads perfectly.
A magnifying-glass will make the difference
more evident. In using quicksilver, be careful that none of it falls on gold or silver coins,
or jewellery, or plate, or on the ornamental
gilding on book-covers. It will do serious
damage.

Plateau's Experiment.

To perform this with very great perfection requires much care and trouble. It is easy to succeed up to a certain point. Pour into a clean bottle about a table-spoonful of salad-oil, and pour upon it a mixture of nine parts by volume spirits of wine (not methylated spirits), and seven parts of water. Shake up and leave for a day if necessary, when it will be found that the oil has settled together by itself. Fill a tumbler with the same mixture of spirit and water, and then with a fine glass pipe, dipping about half-way down, slowly introduce a very little water. This will make the liquid below a little heavier. Dip into the oil a pipe and take out a little by closing the upper end with the finger, and carefully drop this into the tumbler. If it goes to the bottom, a little more water is required in the lower half of the tumbler. If by chance it will not sink at all, a little more spirit is wanted in the upper half. At last the oil will just float in the middle of the mixture. More can then be added, taking care to prevent it from touching the sides. If the liquid below is ever so little heavier, and the liquid above ever so little lighter than oil, the drop of oil perhaps as large as a halfpenny will be almost perfectly round. It will not appear round if seen through the glass, because the glass magnifies it sideways, but not up and down, as may be seen by holding a coin in the liquid just above it. To see the drop in its true shape the vessel must either be a globe, or one side must be made of flat glass.

Spinning the oil so as to throw off a ring is not material, but if the reader can contrive to fix a disc about the size of a threepenny-piece upon a straight wire, and spin it round without shaking it, then he will see the ring break off, and either return if the rotation is quickly stopped, or else break up into three or four perfect little balls. The disc should be wetted with oil before being dipped into the mixture of spirit and water.

A Good Mixture for Soap-Bubbles.

Common yellow soap is far better than most of the fancy soaps, which generally contain a little soap and a lot of rubbish. Castille

soap is very good, and this may be obtained
from any chemist.

Bubbles blown with soap and water alone
do not last long enough for many of the
experiments described, though they may sometimes be made to succeed. Plateau added
glycerine, which greatly improves the lasting
quality. The glycerine should be pure; common glycerine is not good, but Price's answers
perfectly. The water should be pure distilled
water, but if this is not available, clean rain-
water will do. Do not choose the first that runs
from a roof after a spell of dry weather, but
wait till it has rained for some time, the water
that then runs off is very good, especially if
the roof is blue slate or glass. If fresh rain-
water is not to be had, the softest water should
be employed that can be obtained. Instead
-of Castille soap, Plateau found that a pure
soap prepared from olive-oil is still better.
This is called oleate of soda. It should be
obtained freshly prepared from a manufactur-
ing chemist. Old, dry stuff that has been
kept a long time is not so good. I have
always used a modification of Plateau's for-
mula, which Professors Reinold and Rücker

found to answer so well. They used less glycerine than Plateau. It is best made as follows. Fill a clean stoppered bottle three-quarters full of water. Add one-fortieth part of its weight of oleate of soda, which will probably float on the water. Leave it for a day, when the oleate of soda will be dissolved. Nearly fill up the bottle with Price's glycerine and shake well, or pour it into another clean bottle and back again several times. Leave the bottle, stoppered of course, for about a week in a dark place. Then with a syphon, that is, a bent glass tube which will reach to the bottom inside and still further outside, draw off the clear liquid from the scum which will have collected at the top. Add one or two drops of strong liquid ammonia to every pint of the liquid. Then carefully keep it in a stoppered bottle in a dark place. Do not get out this stock bottle every time a bubble is to be blown, but have a small working bottle. Never put any back into the stock. In making the liquid *do not warm or filter it*. Either will spoil it. Never leave the stoppers out of the bottles or allow the liquid to be exposed to the air more than is necessary. This liquid is still perfectly good after two years' keeping. I have given these directions very fully, not because I feel sure that all the details are essential, but because it exactly describes the way I happen to make it, and because I have never found any other solution so good. Castille soap, Price's glycerine, and rain-water will almost certainly answer every purpose, and the same proportions will probably be found to work well.

Rings for Bubbles.

These may be made of any kind of wire. I have used tinned iron about one-twentieth of an inch in diameter. The joint should be smoothly soldered without lumps. If soldering is a difficulty, then use the thinnest wire that is stiff enough to support the bubbles steadily, and make the joint by twisting the end of the wire round two or three times. Rings two inches in diameter are convenient. I have seen that dipping the rings in melted paraffin is recommended, but I have not found any advantage from this. The nicest material for the light rings is thin aluminium wire, about as thick as a fine pin (No. 26 to 30,

K

B. W. G.), and as this cannot be soldered, the ends must be twisted. If this is not to be had, very fine wire, nearly as fine as a hair (No. 36, B. W. G.), of copper or of any other metal, will answer. The rings should be wetted with the soap mixture before a bubble is placed upon them, and must always be well washed and dried when done with.

Threads in Ring.

There is no difficulty in showing these experiments. The ring with the thread may be dipped in the soap solution, or stroked across with the edge of a piece of paper or india-rubber sheet that has been dipped in the liquid, so as to form a film on both sides of the thread. A needle that has also been wetted with the soap may be used to show that the threads are loose. The same needle held for a moment in a candle-flame supplies a convenient means of breaking the film.

Blow out Candle with Soap-Bubble.

For this, the bubble should be blown on the end of a short wide pipe, spread out at one end to give a better hold for the bubble.

The tin funnel supplied with an ordinary gazogene answers perfectly. This should be washed before it is used again for filling the gazogene.

Bubbles balanced against one another.

These experiments are most conveniently made on a small scale. Pieces of thin brass tube, three-eighths or half an inch in diameter, are suitable. It is best to have pieces of apparatus, specially prepared with taps, for easily and quickly stopping the air from leaving either bubble, and for putting the two bubbles into communication when required. It should not be difficult to contrive to perform the experiments, using india-rubber connecting tubes, pinched with spring clips to take the place of taps. There is one little detail which just makes the difference between success and failure. This is to supply a mouth-piece for blowing the bubble, made of glass tube, which has been drawn out so fine that these little bubbles cannot be blown out suddenly by accident. It is very difficult, otherwise, to adjust the quantity of air in such small bubbles with any accuracy. In balancing a spherical against a cylindrical bubble, the short piece of tube, into which the air is supplied, must be made so that it can be easily moved to or from a fixed piece of the same size closed at the other end. Then the two ends of the short tube must have a film spread over them with a piece of paper, or india-rubber, but there must be *no* film stretched across the end of the fixed tube. The two tubes must at first be near together, until the spherical bubble has been formed. They may then be separated gradually more and more, and air blown in so as to keep the sides of the cylinder straight, until the cylinder is sufficiently long to be nearly unstable. It will then far more evidently show, by its change of form, than it would if it were short, when the pressure due to the spherical bubble exactly balances that due to a cylindrical one. If the shadow of the bubbles, or an image formed by a lens on a screen, is then measured, it will be found that the sphere has a diameter which is very accurately double that of the cylinder.

Thaumatrope for showing the Formation and Oscillations of Drops.

The experiment showing the formation of water-drops can be very perfectly imitated, and the movements actually made visible, without any necessity for using liquids at all, by simply converting Fig. 35 (at end of book) into the old-fashioned instrument called a thaumatrope. What will then be seen is a true representation, because the forms in the figure are copies of a series of photographs taken from the moving drops at the rate of forty-three photographs in two seconds.[1]

Obtain a piece of good cardboard as large as the figure, and having brushed it all over on one side with thin paste, lay the figure upon it, and press it down evenly. Place it upon a table, and cover it with a few thicknesses of blotting-paper, and lay over all a flat piece of board large enough to cover it. Weights sufficient to keep it all flat may be added. This must be left all night at least, until the card is quite dry, or else it will curl

[1] For particulars see *Philosophical Magazine*, September 1890.

up and be useless. Now with a sharp chisel
or knife, but a chisel if possible, cut out the
forty-three slits near the edge, accurately
following the outline indicated in black and
white, and keeping the slits as narrow as
possible. Then cut a hole in the middle, so as
to fit the projecting part of a sewing-machine
cotton-reel, and fasten the cotton-reel on the
side away from the figure with glue or small
nails. It must be fixed exactly in the middle.
The edge should of course be cut down to
the outside of the black rim.

Now having found a pencil or other rod
on which the cotton-reel will freely turn, use
this as an axle, and holding the disc up in
front of a looking-glass, and in a good light,
slowly and steadily make it turn round. The
image of the disc seen through the slit in the
looking-glass will then perfectly represent every
feature of the growing and falling drop. As
the drop grows it will gradually become too
heavy to be supported, a waist will then begin
to form which will rapidly get narrower, until
the drop at last breaks away. It will be seen
to continue its fall until it has disappeared in the
liquid below, but it has not mixed with this,

and so it will presently appear again, having
bounced out of the liquid. As it falls it will
be seen to vibrate as the result of the sudden
release from the one-sided pull. The neck
which was drawn out will meanwhile have
gathered itself in the form of a little drop, which
will then be violently hit by the oscillations of
the remaining pendant drop above, and driven
down. The pendant drop will be seen to
vibrate and grow at the same time, until it
again breaks away as before, and so the
phenomena are repeated.

In order to perfectly reproduce the experiment, the axle should be firmly held upon a
stand, and the speed should not exceed one
turn in two seconds.

The effect is still more real if a screen is
placed between the disc and the mirror, which
will only allow one of the drops to be seen.

Water-drops in Paraffin and Bisulphide of Carbon.

All that was said in describing the Plateau
experiment applies here. Perfectly spherical
and large drops of water can be formed in a

mixture so made that the lower parts are very
little heavier, and the upper parts very little
lighter, than water. The addition of bisulphide
of carbon makes the mixture heavier. This
liquid—bisulphide of carbon—is very dangerous, and has a most dreadful smell, so that it
had better not be brought into the house. The
form of a hanging drop, and the way in which
it breaks off, can be seen if water is used in
paraffin alone, but it is much more evident
if a little bisulphide of carbon is mixed with
the paraffin, so that water will sink slowly
in the mixture. Pieces of glass tube, open
at both ends from half an inch to one inch
in diameter, show the action best. Having
poured some water coloured blue into a glass
vessel, and covered it to a depth of several
inches with paraffin, or the paraffin mixture,
dip the pipe down into the water, having first
closed the upper end with the thumb or the
palm of the hand. On then removing the
hand, the water will rush up inside the tube.
Again close the upper end as before, and raise
the tube until the lower end is well above the
water, though still immersed in the paraffin.
Then allow air to enter the pipe very slowly

by just rolling the thumb the least bit to one side. The water will escape slowly and form a large growing drop, the size of which, before it breaks away, will depend on the density of the mixture and the size of the tube.

To form a water cylinder in the paraffin the tube must be filled with water as before, but the upper end must now be left open. Then when all is quiet the tube is to be rather rapidly withdrawn in the direction of its own length, when the water which was within it will be left behind in form of a cylinder, surrounded by the paraffin. It will then break up into spheres so slowly, in the case of a large tube, that the operation can be watched. The depth of paraffin should be quite ten times the diameter of the tube.

To make bubbles of water in the paraffin, the tube must be dipped down into the water with the upper end open all the time, so that the tube is mostly filled with paraffin. It must then be closed for a moment above and raised till the end is completely out of the water. Then if air is allowed to enter slowly, and the tube is gently raised, bubbles of water filled with paraffin will be formed which can

be made to separate from the pipe, like soap-
bubbles from a "churchwarden," by a suitable
sudden movement. If a number of water-
drops are floating in the paraffin in the pipe,
and this can be easily arranged, then the
bubbles made will contain possibly a number
of other drops, or even other bubbles. A very
little bisulphide of carbon poured carefully
down a pipe will form a heavy layer above
the water, on which these compound bubbles
will remain floating.

Cylindrical bubbles of water in paraffin may
be made by dipping the pipe down into the
water and withdrawing it quickly without ever
closing the top at all. These break up into
spherical bubbles in the same way that the
cylinder of liquid broke up into spheres of
liquid.

Beaded Spider-webs.

These are found in the spiral part of the
webs of all the geometrical spiders. The
beautiful geometrical webs may be found out
of doors in abundance in the autumn, or in
green-houses at almost any time of the year.
To mount these webs so that the beads may

be seen, take a small flat ring of any material, or a piece of card-board with a hole cut out with a gun-wad cutter, or otherwise. Smear the face of the ring, or the card, with a very little strong gum. Choose a freshly-made web, and then pass the ring, or the card, across the web so that some of the spiral web (not the central part of the web) remains stretched across the hole. This must be done without touching or damaging the pieces that are stretched across, except at their ends. The beads are too small to be seen with the naked eye. A strong magnifying-glass, or a low power microscope, will show the beads and their marvellous regularity. The beads on the webs of very young spiders are not so regular as those on spiders that are fully grown. Those beautiful beads, easily visible to the naked eye, on spider lines in the early morning of an autumn day, are not made by the spider, but are simply dew. They very perfectly show the spherical form of small water-drops.

Photographs of Water-jets.

These are easily taken by the method
described by Mr. Chichester Bell. The flash
of light is produced by a short spark from
a few Leyden-jars. The fountain, or jet, should
be five or six feet away from the spark, and
the photographic plate should be held as close
to the stream of water as is possible without
touching. The shadow is then so definite that
the photograph, when taken, may be examined
with a powerful lens, and will still appear sharp.
Any rapid dry plate will do. The room, of
course, must be quite dark when the plate is
placed in position, and the spark then made.
The regular breaking up of the jet may be
effected by sound produced in almost any way.
The straight jet, of which Fig. 41 is a representation, magnified about three and a quarter
times, was regularly broken up by simply
whistling to it with a key. The fountains were
broken up regularly by fastening the nozzle to
one end of a long piece of wood clamped at
the end to the stand of a tuning-fork, which
was kept sounding by electrical means. An
ordinary tuning-fork, made to rest when sound-

ing against the wooden support of the nozzle, will answer quite as well, but is not quite so convenient.   The jet will break up best to certain notes, but it may be tuned to a great extent by altering the size of the orifice or the pressure of the water, or both.

Fountain and Sealing-wax.

It is almost impossible to fail over this very striking yet simple experiment.   A fountain of almost any size, at any rate between one-fiftieth and a quarter of an inch in the smooth part, and up to eight feet high, will cease to scatter when the sealing-wax is rubbed with flannel and held a few feet away.   A suitable size of fountain is one about four feet high, coming from an orifice anywhere near one-sixteenth of an inch in diameter.   The nozzle should be inclined so that the water falls slightly on one side.   The sealing-wax may be electrified by being rubbed on the coat-sleeve, or on a piece of fur or flannel which is *dry*.   It will then make little pieces of paper or cork dance, but it will still act on the fountain when it has ceased to produce any visible effect on pieces of paper, or even on a delicate gold-leaf electroscope.

Bouncing Water-jets.

This beautiful experiment of Lord Rayleigh's requires a little management to make it work in a satisfactory manner. Take a piece of quill-glass tube and draw it out to a very slight extent (see a former note), so as to make a neck about one-eighth of an inch in diameter at the narrowest part. Break the tube just at this place, after first nicking it there with a file. Connect each of these tubes by means of an india-rubber pipe, or otherwise, with a supply of water in a bottle, and pinch the tubes with a screw-clip until two equal jets of water are formed. So hold the nozzles that these meet in their smooth portions at every small angle. They will then for a short time bounce away from one another without mixing. If the air is very dusty, if the water is not clean, or if air-bubbles are carried along in the pipes, the two jets will at once join together. In the arrangement that I used in the lantern, the two nozzles were nearly horizontal, one was about half an inch above the other, and they were very slightly converging. They were fastened in their position by melting upon them a little sealing-wax. India-rubber pipes connected them with two bottles about six inches above them, and screw-clips were used to regulate the supply. One of the bottles was made to stand on three pieces of sealing-wax to electrically insulate it, and the corresponding nozzle was only held by its sealing-wax fastening. The water in the bottles had been filtered, and one was coloured blue. If these precautions are taken, the jets will remain distinct quite long enough, but are instantly caused to recombine by a piece of electrified sealing-wax six or eight feet away. They may be separated again by touching the water issuing near one nozzle with the finger, which deflects it; on quietly removing the finger the jet takes up its old position and bounces off the other as before. They can thus be separated and made to combine ten or a dozen times in a minute.

Fountain and Intermittent Light.

This can be successfully shown to a large
number of people at once only by using an
electric arc, but there is no occasion to produce
this light if not more than one person at a time
wishes to see the evolution of the drops.   It is
then merely necessary to make the fountain play
in front of a bright background such as the
sky, to break it up with a tuning-fork or other
musical sound as described, and then to look
at it through a card disc equally divided near
the edge into spaces about two or three inches
wide, with a hole about one-eighth of an inch
in diameter between each pair of spaces.   A
disc of card five inches in diameter, with six
equidistant holes half an inch from the edge,
answers well.   The disc must be made to
spin by any means very regularly at such
a speed that the tuning-fork, or stretched
string if this be used, when looked at through
the holes, appears quiet, or nearly quiet, when
made to vibrate.   The separate drops will
then be seen, and everything described in the
preceding pages, and a great deal more, will
be evident.   This is one of the most fascin-

ating experiments, and it is well worth while to make an effort to succeed. The little motor that I used is one of Cuttriss and Co.'s P. I. motors, which are very convenient for experiments of this kind. It was driven by four Grove's cells. These make it rotate too fast, but the speed can be reduced by moving the brushes slightly towards the position used for reversing the motor, until the speed is almost exactly right. It is best to arrange that it goes only just too fast, then the speed can be perfectly regulated by a very light pressure of the finger on the end of the axle.

Mr. Chichester Bell's Singing Water-jet.

For these experiments a very fine hole about one seventy-fifth of an inch in diameter is most suitable. To obtain this, Mr. Bell holds the end of a quill-glass tube in a blow-pipe flame, and constantly turns it round and round until the end is almost entirely closed up. He then suddenly and forcibly blows into the pipe. Out of several nozzles made in this way, some are sure to do well. Lord Rayleigh makes nozzles generally by cementing to the

L

end of a glass (or metal) pipe a piece of thin
sheet metal in which a hole of the required
size has been made. The water pressure should
be produced by a head of about fifteen feet.
The water must be quite free from dust and
from air-bubbles. This may be effected by
making it pass through a piece of tube stuffed
full of flannel, or cotton-wool, or something of
the kind to act as a filter. There should be
a yard or so of good black india-rubber tube,
about one-eighth of an inch in diameter inside,
between the filter and the nozzle. It is best
not to take the water direct from the water-
main, but from a cistern about fifteen feet
above the nozzle. If no cistern is available,
a pail of water taken up-stairs, with a pipe
coming down, is an excellent substitute, and
this has the further advantage that the head
of water can be easily changed so as to arrive
at the best result.

The rest of the apparatus is very simple.
It is merely necessary to stretch and tie over
the end of a tube about half an inch in
diameter a piece of thin india-rubber sheet,
cut from an air-ball that has·not been blown
out. The tube, which may be of metal or of

glass, may either be fastened to a heavy foot, in which case a side tube must be joined to it, as in Fig. 47, or it may be open at both ends and be held in a clamp. It is well to put a cone of card-board on the open end (Fig. 48), if the sound is to be heard by many at a time. If the experimenter alone wishes to hear as well as possible when faint sounds are produced, he should carry a piece of smooth india-rubber tube about half an inch in diameter from the open end to his ear. This, however, would nearly deafen him with such loud noises as the tick of a watch.

Bubbles and Ether.

Experiments with ether must be performed with great care, because, like the bisulphide of carbon, it is dangerously inflammable. The bottle of ether must never be brought near a light. If a large quantity is spilled, the heavy vapour is apt to run along the floor and ignite at a fire, even on the other side of a room. Any vessel may be filled with the vapour of ether by merely pouring the liquid upon a piece of blotting-paper reaching up to the level of the edge. Very little is required, say half a wine-glassful, for a basin that would hold a gallon or more. In a draughty place the vapour will be lost in a short time. Bubbles can be set to float upon the vapour without any difficulty. They may be removed in five or ten seconds by means of one of the small light rings with a handle, provided that the ring is wetted with the soap solution and has *no* film stretched across it. If taken to a light at a safe distance the bubble will immediately burst into a blaze. If a neighbouring light is not close down to the table, but well up above the jar on a stand, it may be near with but little risk. To show the burning vapour, the same wide tube that was used to blow out the candle will answer well. The pear shape of the bubble, owing to its increased weight after being held in the vapour for ten or fifteen seconds, is evident enough on its removal, but the falling stream of heavy vapour, which comes out again afterwards, can only be shown if its shadow is cast upon a screen by means of a bright light.

Experiment with Internal Bubbles.

For these experiments, next to a good solu-tion, the pipe is of the greatest importance. A "churchwarden" is no use. A glass pipe $\frac{5}{16}$ inch in diameter at the mouth is best. If this is merely a tube bent near the end through a right angle, moisture condensed in the tube will in time run down and destroy the bubble occasionally, which is very annoy-ing in a difficult experiment. I have made for myself the pipe of which Fig. 67 is a full size representation, and I do not think that it is possible to improve upon this. Those who are not glass-blowers will be able, with the help of cork, to make a pipe with a trap as shown in Fig. 68, which is as good, except in appearance and handiness.

In knocking bubbles together to show that they do not touch, care must be taken to avoid letting either bubble meet any projection in the other, such as the wire ring, or a heavy drop of liquid. Either will instantly destroy the two bubbles. There is also a limit to the violence which may be used, which experience will soon indicate.

In pushing a bubble through a ring smaller than itself, by means of a flat film on another ring, it is important that the bubble should not be too large; but a larger bubble can be pushed through than would be expected. It is not so easy to push it up as down because of the ·heavy drop of liquid, which it is difficult to completely drain away.

To blow one bubble inside another, the first, as large as an average orange, should be blown on the lower side of a horizontal ring. A light

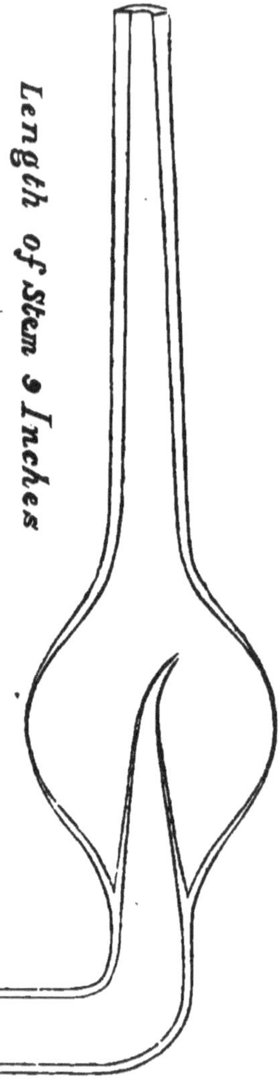

Length of Stem 9 Inches

Fig. 67.

wire ring should then be hung on to this bubble to slightly pull it out of shape. For this purpose thin aluminium rings are hardly heavy enough, and so either a heavier metal should

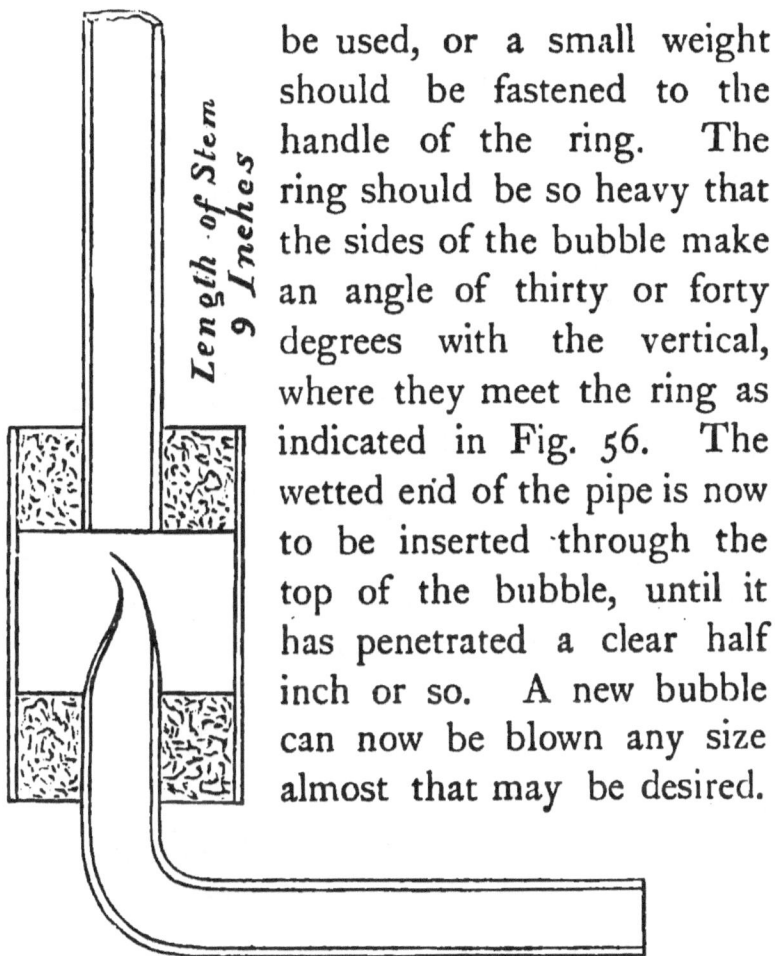

be used, or a small weight should be fastened to the handle of the ring. The ring should be so heavy that the sides of the bubble make an angle of thirty or forty degrees with the vertical, where they meet the ring as indicated in Fig. 56. The wetted end of the pipe is now to be inserted through the top of the bubble, until it has penetrated a clear half inch or so. A new bubble can now be blown any size almost that may be desired.

Fig. 68.

To remove the pipe a slow motion will be fatal, because it will raise the inner bubble until it and the outer one both meet the pipe at the same place. This will bring them into true contact. On the other hand, a violent jerk will almost certainly produce too great a disturbance. A rather rapid motion, or a slight jerk, is all that is required. It is advisable before passing the pipe up through the lower ring, so as to touch the inner bubble, and so drain away the heavy drop, to steady this with the other hand. The superfluous liquid can then be drained from both bubbles simultaneously. Care must be taken after this that the inner bubble is not allowed to come against either wire ring, nor must the pipe be passed through the side where the two bubbles are very close together. To peel off the lower ring it should be pulled down a very little way and then inclined to one side. The peeling will then start more readily, but as soon as it has begun the ring should be raised so as not to make the peeling too rapid, otherwise the final jerk, when it leaves the lower ring, will be too much for the bubbles to withstand.

Bubbles coloured with fluorescine, or uranine, do not show their brilliant fluorescence unless sunlight or electric light is concentrated upon them with a lens or mirror. The quantity of dye required is so small that it may be difficult to take little enough. As much as can be picked up on the last eighth of an inch of a pointed pen-knife will be, roughly speaking, enough for a wine-glassful of the soap solution. If the quantity is increased beyond something like the proportion stated, the fluorescence becomes less and very soon disappears. The best quantity can be found in a few minutes by trial.

To blow bubbles containing either coal-gas or air, or a mixture of the two, the most convenient plan is to have a small T-shaped glass tube which can be joined by one arm of the T to the blow-pipe by means of a short piece of india-rubber tube, and be connected by its vertical limb with a sufficient length of india-rubber pipe, one-eighth of an inch in diameter inside, to reach to the floor, after which it may be connected by any kind of pipe with the gas supply. The gas can be stopped either by pinching the india-rubber tube with the left hand, if that is at liberty, or by treading on it if both hands are occupied. Meanwhile air can be blown in by the other arm of the T, and the end closed by the tongue when gas alone is required. This

end of the tube should be slightly spread out
when hot by rapidly pushing into it the *cold*
tang of a file, and twisting it at the same time,
so that it may be lightly held by the teeth
without fear of slipping.

If a light T-piece or so great a length of
small india-rubber tube cannot be obtained,
then the mouth must be removed from the pipe
and the india-rubber tube slipped in when air
is to be changed for gas. This makes the
manipulation more difficult, but all the experiments, except the one with three bubbles, can
be so carried out.

The pipe must in every case be made to
enter the highest point of a bubble in order
to start an internal one. If it is pushed
horizontally through the side, the inner bubble
is sure to break. If the inner bubble is being
blown with gas, it will soon tend to rise. The
pipe must then be turned over in such a
manner that the inner bubble does not creep
along it, and so meet the outer one where
penetrated by the pipe. A few trials will show
what is meant. The inner bubble may then
be allowed to rest against the top of the outer
one while being enlarged. When it is desired

after withdrawing the pipe to blow more air
or gas into either the inner or the outer bubble,
it is not safe after inserting the pipe again to
begin to blow at once; the film which is now
stretched across the mouth of the pipe will
probably become a third bubble, and this, under
the circumstances, is almost certain to cause a
failure. An instantaneous withdrawal of the air
destroys this film by drawing it into the pipe.
Air or gas may then be blown without danger.

If the same experiment is performed upon
a light ring with cotton and paper attached,
the left hand will be occupied in holding this
ring, and then the gas must be controlled by
the foot, or by a friend. The light ring
should be quite two inches in diameter. If,
when the inner bubble has begun to carry
away the ring, &c., the paper is caught hold
of, it is possible, by a judicious pull, to cause
the two bubbles to leave the ring and so
escape into the air one inside the other. For
this purpose the smallest ring that will carry
the paper should be used. With larger rings
the same effect may be produced by inclining
the ring, and so allowing the outer bubble to
peel off, or by placing the mouth of the pipe

against the ring and blowing a third bubble
in real contact with the ring and the outer
bubble. This will assist the peeling process.

To blow three bubbles, one inside the other
two, is more difficult. The following plan I
have found to be fairly certain. First blow
above the ring a bubble the size of a large
orange. Then take a small ring about an inch
in diameter, with a straight wire coming down
from one side to act as a handle, and after
wetting it with the solution, pass it carefully
up through the fixed ring so that the small
ring is held well inside the bubble. Now
pass the pipe, freshly dipped in the solution,
into the outer or No. 1 bubble until it is
quite close to the small ring, and begin to
blow the No. 2 bubble. This must be started
with the pipe almost in contact with the inner
ring, as the film on this ring would destroy
a bubble that had attained any size. Withdraw the pipe, dip it into the liquid, and
insert it into the inner bubble, taking care
to keep these two bubbles from meeting anywhere. Now blow a large gas-bubble, which
may rest against the top of No. 2 while it is
growing. No. 2 may now rest against the

top of No. 1 without danger. Remove pipe from No. 3 by gently lowering it, and let some gas into No. 2 to make it lighter, and at the same time diminish the pressure between Nos. 2 and 3. Presently the small ring can be peeled off No. 2 and removed altogether. But if there is a difficulty in accomplishing this, withdraw the pipe from No. 2 and blow air into No. 1 to enlarge it, which will make the process easier. Then remove the pipe from No. 1. The three bubbles are now resting one inside the other. By blowing a fourth bubble, as described above, against the fixed ring, No. 1 bubble will peel off, and the three will float away. No. 1 can, while peeling, be transferred to a light wire ring from which paper, &c. are suspended. This description sounds complicated, but after a little practice the process can be carried out almost with certainty in far less time than it takes to describe it; in fact, so quickly can it be done, and so simple does it appear, that no one would suppose that so many details had to be attended to.

Bubbles and Electricity.

These experiments are on the whole the most difficult to perform successfully. The following details should be sufficient to prevent failure. Two rings are formed at the end of a pair of wires about six inches long in the straight part. About one inch at the opposite end from the ring is turned down at a right angle. These turned-down ends rest in two holes drilled vertically in a non-conductor such as ebonite, about two or three inches apart. Then if all is right the two rings are horizontal and at the same level, and they may be moved towards or away from one another. Separate them a few inches, and blow a bubble above or below each, making them nearly the same size. Then bring the two rings nearer together until the bubbles just, and only just, rest against one another. Though they may be hammered together without joining, they will not remain long resting in this position, as the convex surfaces can readily squeeze out the air. The ebonite should not be perfectly warm and dry, for it is then sure to be electrified, and this will give trouble. It must not be wet, because then it will conduct, and the sealing-wax will produce no result. If it has been used as the support for the rings for some of the previous experiments, it will have been sufficiently splashed by the bursting of bubbles to be in the best condition. It must, however, be well wiped occasionally.

A stick of sealing-wax should be held in readiness under the arm, in a fold or two of *dry* flannel or fur. If the wax is very strongly electrified, it is apt to be far too powerful, and to cause the bubbles, when it is presented to them, to destroy each other. A feeble electrification is sufficient; then the instant it is exposed the bubbles coalesce. The wax may be brought so near one bubble in which another one is resting, that it pulls them to one side, but the inner one is screened from electrical action by the outer one. It is important not to bring the wax very near, as in that case the bubble will be pulled so far as to touch it, and so be broken. The wetting of the wax will make further electrification very uncertain. In showing the difference between an inner and an outer bubble, the same remarks with regard to undue pressure, electrification, or loss of time apply. I have generally found that it is advisable in this experiment not to drain the drops from both the bubbles, as their weight seems to steady them ; the external bubble may be drained, and if it is not too large, the process of electrically joining the outer bubbles, without injury to the inner one, may be repeated many times. I once caused eight or nine single bubbles to unite with the outer one of a' pair in succession before it became too unwieldy for more accessions to be possible.

It would_ be going outside my subject to say anything about the management of lanterns. I may, however, state that while the experiments with the small bubbles are best projected with a lens upon the screen, the larger bubbles described in the last lecture can only be projected by their shadows. For this purpose the condensing lens is removed, and the bare light alone made use of. An electric arc is far preferable to a lime-light, both because the shadows are sharper, and because the colours are so much more brilliant. No oil lamp would answer, even if the light were sufficient in quantity, because the flame would be far too large to cast a sharp shadow.

In these hints, which have in themselves required a rather formidable chapter, I have given all the details, so far as I am able, which a considerable experience has shown to be necessary for the successful performance of the experiments in public. The hints will I hope materially assist those who are not in the habit of carrying out experiments, but who may wish to perform them for their own satisfaction. Though people who are not experimentalists may consider that the hints are overburdened with detail, it is probable that in repeating the experiments they will find here and there, in spite of all my care to provide against unforeseen difficulties, that more detail would have been desirable.

Though it is unusual to conclude such a book as this with the fullest directions for

M

carrying out the experiments described, I believe that the innovation in the present instance is good, more especially because many of the experiments require none of the elaborate apparatus which so often is necessary.

THE END.

Richard Clay & Sons, Limited, London & Bungay.